For Steph

Love Changes Everything...

Jill Dunsell

Winters' Season

Book Three: Chicago Series
Jennifer Driscoll

Copyright © 2018 by Jennifer Driscoll
Cover Design: Rhonda Duffy

ISBN: 978-1-7326238-1-1 (Print)
ISBN: 978-1-7326238-0-4 (eBook)

For the incredible moms in my life...

For my own mom, Rose, who raised me with strength, independence, and grace.

For my mother-in-law, Mary Lue, whose enthusiasm started me down this journey and whose support has never wavered, in good times and in bad.

For my physician moms, Mattawan moms, book club moms, breast cancer moms, writer moms, dinner club moms, stay-at-home moms...

You are all things to your families and not only my friends, but my everyday inspirations.

You can't go back and change the beginning,
but you can start where you are and change the
ending.

-C.S. Lewis

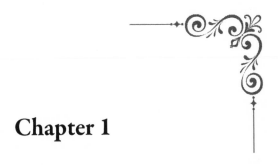

Chapter 1

"HOW MUCH OF A TERROR was he tonight?" Molly pushed through her apartment door, arms filled with catering trays and a small bakery box tilting forward, on the verge of frosting her entire entryway, tiny as it was. Abby, her neighbor and frequent babysitter to her son, Sam, jumped up to catch the falling box. "I think he's had more sugar in the last week since Christmas than he's had in his whole life."

"Oh, he was no trouble at all. He never is." Abby waved her hand in the air, swiping away Molly's guilt. "My kids always had sugar. We didn't know any different back then. They turned out just fine. Well, Matt had that minor thing with the police, but you know, mostly, he came out fine." She laughed to herself. "Sam and I made mac n' cheese and watched the Transformers...again. If I have a complaint, it's that he prefers robots over handsome superheroes. I could use a little more Hemsworth in my life." She laughed and rolled her eyes. "He gave me a little hassle about reading before bed, but we settled on the new Bumble Bee book he got under the tree, and he was out before Optimus saved the day."

"You're the best, Abby. I'm afraid that I have to pay you with food tonight. Lots of leftovers from my catering gig. Take that top one." Molly pointed to a light-pink bakery box. "It has those little tea cakes that are your favorite."

Abby picked up the box from the counter and inhaled the sweet scent. "Not turning that down. I always like staying with Sam. You know you don't have to pay me." She took a bite of the cake. "I take that

1

back. You'll pay in cake from now on." She closed her eyes and smiled, savoring the sweet nugget.

"If you're good with it, I'm just going to change my clothes quick and run some food downstairs. I saw Ken on the back steps. It's so freaking cold out there tonight." She'd stripped off her winter coat, hat, and gloves. "I've got to peel myself out of this shirt first, though. I made pasta with meat sauce tonight, and I think it will be permanently pink if I don't get some stain wash on it."

"I'll stay until you come back up. Finish watching my show and enjoy a little more cake." Abby wiggled her eyebrows and sat back on the well-worn couch with the remote control.

"Thanks, Abby. I shouldn't be too long." After finding her favorite pair of yoga pants and an oversized t-shirt, soaking her work shirt in the bathroom sink, picking up two towels from the hallway floor, kissing a sleeping Sam's head, and putting her cold weather gear back on, she padded down the back stairs to the rear entrance of her building.

"Ken, how are you?" She sat on the cold concrete step next to him and handed over a plate of pasta, garlic bread, and some broccoli. "Nourishment." His beard had filled in, giving him the appearance of a fuller face. His dark-brown eyes were still sunken, though. She knew he probably hadn't eaten today.

"Jolly Molly. I thank you kindly." Even his voice seemed weaker than when she had seen him last.

"I was hoping to find you out here. Well, really, I was hoping you were warm somewhere, but I did want to catch up with you. I have good news and bad news."

"Hit me with the good news. Life's too short for bad news first."

"Ah, philosopher Ken on my doorstep tonight. Well, you're eating the good news. I had lots of leftovers from my event tonight. Will you be headed over to the shelter? I can send this whole tray with you."

"Yeah, I'll take that over. The guys will appreciate it." She watched him shovel in the food. He barely paused between bites to ask, "And what's the bad news?"

"I'm going away for a few days. I've got to go to a friend's wedding. Can I give you some money to get you by while I'm gone?"

"No, love. The food is perfect. Do you need a plus-one though? There was a time in my life when I looked mighty fine in a suit." Molly giggled as she thought of the looks she might get if she brought her homeless friend Ken to millionaire surgeon CJ Montgomery's wedding in Saint Kitts.

"Sorry, friend. I'm sure you would look great, but I've actually got the cutest plus-one ever. He's got my heart." She tucked her hands under her armpits. *Dang, it's cold!*

"Worth a shot, pretty girl!" Ken handed her the now empty plate and fork. "I'll take this tray to the shelter. Let them know we won't be seeing more for a bit. Happy for you, girl. You deserve a nice vacation, always taking care of us and that boy of yours. Go have fun! Get your party on!"

She laughed at the little dance he did, shaking his hips as he stood up. "I suspect my presence is considered more helpful babysitter than essential to the fun, but I've never been out of the country before, so I'm going to make the most of it anyway. Maybe I'll have some new recipes to try out on you when I get back."

He lifted the food tray from the step and set it on his cart before he pushed off in the direction of the homeless shelter three blocks to the east. "I love you, Jolly Molly. Come back safe."

She rested her arms and chin on her bent knees. "I love you too," she whispered more to herself than him. "Be safe while I'm gone."

Shivering, she returned to the warmth of her apartment. Abby left her to finish laundry, packing, bill paying, business planning, and clean-up duty from the evening. Sam, of course, slept through it all. She wouldn't have had it any other way. A little more help around the house

3

would have been nice, though, along with a little extra spending cash. She'd throw in a Miele range and a hot hunk to rub her feet at the end of the day if she were allowed to dream. Not that she permitted herself that kind of fantasy.

She and Sam were doing ok. Sam seemed to grow every time he was away from her for more than a few hours. At this rate, he would probably be taller than her by morning. He'd turned seven, to her utter astonishment, just a week after she'd turned twenty-three.

Seven tumultuous years together, always together. Sam's dad, Eric, the worst choice she'd ever made in her life, remained in prison – safely out of their lives for the foreseeable future, not that he'd wanted to be with her after she had told him about the pregnancy. In hindsight, it was the best decision Eric had ever made for her.

He'd come back to town, tried in vain to blackmail her best friend Drew, and vandalized Drew's shop and his beautiful boats. That was before Eric had been caught in a gambling scheme and put away for that too. She'd never pictured this life, never dreamed of quiet nights at home in her twenties, never wanted to be a single mom with a story to tell. But here they were, and they were doing ok.

She continued to work at the bookstore when they had a shift for her, which filled in the gaps but wasn't going to pay for that high-end range or jet-setting international vacations any time soon. She took on small catering events whenever she could. She had been getting some good word of mouth from the few events she'd done. Tonight's gala had been a Moose Lodge anniversary dinner. Not exactly Chicago-surgeon-socialite-marries-high-school-sweetheart-in-Saint-Kitts stuff, but a job was a job. She'd be one of the last to arrive for the wedding because of it. Well, she wasn't family, despite the invitation to stay at the Montgomery family house on the island. No, she would be there to help her half-sister, Jillian, and Drew with their now mobile nine-month-old twins, maybe cook some family meals, and watch sweethearts say I do, all while taking her son on an amazing island getaway, which she could never have afforded under any other circumstances.

Yeah, they were doing ok. Life had been tough the last few years without her dad, living with the guilt of what he had done, or had tried to do, to Drew and Jillian. Living with the knowledge that he had caused her mom's car accident and taken her from both of her daughters' lives forever. Living with the responsibility of raising Sam with grace, forgiving her dad, and finding peace in knowing her sister, Jillian. She would save the worry for another day. Tomorrow was for celebration.

Her last thoughts were of a hunk waiting in Saint Kitts as she finally dozed off on the couch. It made for a nice dream.

KERRY MONTGOMERY STRODE past the ten-foot wall of windows that led from the boardroom toward his high-rise office inside the Montgomery Shipping building. Despite the hustle he knew was happening inside each of the towers in view, the Chicago skyline appeared to be frozen in place on this desperately cold January day, like icy stalagmites jutting up along the Lake Michigan shore.

Janie pulled up next to him with an update. "Your eleven o'clock canceled, so your schedule is cleared for the rest of the day. Here are the Pattinson Shipping file and those tax documents you requested to take on your trip. Goodness knows why. Really, you should have a proper vacation, Mr. Montgomery. I also have your passport and airport transfer information."

"Did you happen to get Michael to pick us up?" His tone was hopeful. He hadn't seen his friend in at least a year.

"Yes, I spoke to him briefly. I know he is an old friend, but he sure is...casual with his words. Long story short, he'll be there to get you when you land. I also notified the airport that you would be ahead of schedule. The plane is ready when you are." Janie chugged out the updated schedule as she tried to keep up with Kerry Montgomery and his mile-long strides. Winded, she stopped outside of his office. "I'm looking forward to moving in slow motion for the next few days. Why don't any Montgomerys walk at a normal pace around here? You are just like your dad."

"I'm going to pretend you did not just say that. You wound me with your words, Janie."

She laughed at his dramatic fist to his chest.

"Can you also get me the plans the architect sent over for the new plant and the renderings on a flash drive? Also the extra laptop battery. And something to eat?" He gave his most hopeful face to his long-time assistant, the one that always worked on his mom. "Anything is fine."

"Sure. But your plane..."

"The plane will be there. Aren't we waiting for the others? Molly and Sam? And Sunny?"

"I called to let them know you would be ahead of schedule. Molly Winters sounded frazzled and apologetic. Sunny Paulson...not so much."

Kerry muttered to himself as he entered his office, "Sounds about right."

He turned back with a thought. "Janie, maybe send a car for Molly and Sam..."

"Already did," she shouted back toward his open office door as she moved down the hall to grab his lunch.

"She already did," he whispered and nodded his head. "Also sounds about right."

He had squeezed in one more hour of productivity and a less-than-stellar egg salad sandwich on wheat when his car arrived to take him to the airport. His younger brother was getting married this weekend. If you'd have asked him a year ago if CJ would ever take himself off the market in favor of one woman for the rest of his life, he'd have laughed so hard the egg salad would have escaped, but Hailey...Hailey Powers was the exception. She always had been. She'd come back into his life dramatically, no doubt, but he was pretty sure CJ lived life best down in the trenches of humanity, in amongst the drama. He was a trauma surgeon, after all; his career required chaos. Kerry reflected on his peaceful life in the towers of Chicago's loop. The quiet, methodical office that surrounded him seemed just fine by him.

He knew his two younger brothers had never understood why he would want to work here, in a glorified cubicle, and for their dad, no less. But he was also sure that they didn't understand him, not really. They thrived on the creative and the chaos. He loved his work at Montgomery Shipping because it was accomplished strictly by the numbers. In each task, there was a routine, and in each project, the details mattered. Math never required creativity, and it never created chaos. In short, the math never let him down.

Now he was off to his younger brother's wedding. A casual affair at the family home in Saint Kitts where they'd traveled as kids, teenagers, men. Birthdays, Christmases, and now a wedding on the island he had always considered his second home. Janie returned to interrupt his thoughts.

"Your car is here. He has your luggage and garment bag. You have your passport, laptop, and travel case." She pointed to each item with her ballpoint pen as she checked them off the list in her head.

"Either you're channeling my mother right now or you really want me on that plane."

"Oh, go, young man. Give that CJ a big hug for me, and Hailey too. And have a great time with the family. This desk will still be waiting for you when you return."

Kerry took the private elevator down to the lobby and slipped into the black car for the short ride to the private airport. He passed through ticketing and onto the tarmac without issue before greeting the pilot on board. "Thanks for coming back for us, Pete. Everyone else make it in ok at the other end yesterday?"

"All good. We'll be the last flight into the private side today. Pre-flight checks are done. We'll leave as soon as everyone is on board and the safety checks are complete."

"Thanks. I'll go get myself settled."

The family plane had been his father's one true extravagance. Kerry knew that he secretly loved having everyone in the family together as much as his mom did, maybe more. The plane was a means to that end more than a business necessity, not that his dad would ever admit it. It was edging toward ten years old, and as the family grew from marriages and grandchildren, he suspected JP Montgomery was on the lookout for an upgrade.

Kerry waved hello to the flight attendant, Bridget, at the back of the plane as he hung his garment bag in the closet and stashed his travel case on the floor. Pulling out his tattered copy of *Ready Player One*, he thought he could sit near the window and tune out the world for the next four hours, but then Sunny Paulson's massive green sun hat poked through the open boarding door. It practically poked him in the eye when she gave him two air kisses – one near, but not technically on, each cheek.

Sunny epitomized the society set. She would have been a perfect debutant had she been born in the South, except she lacked the sweetness ladies in the South were known for. Her parents and his had been friends since the days of having little cash and even less social clout. As far as he could tell, they had created their wealth together, and it was expected that their children would solidify the arrangement. He hadn't quite figured out a politically correct way to get out of the setup. And he knew Sunny would always take advantage of his kindness, his lack of confrontation, his reluctant friendship.

"Kerry! Hi, love. It's been too long. Why has it been so long? Have you been hiding in your tall tower? Anyway, could you get my bags, hon?" She removed the hat, revealing her trademark platinum-blonde bob. "And could you hang up my coat? Thanks. I've got to freshen up. Be right back."

Kerry handed the coat to Bridget, whom he'd seen rolling her eyes at his exchange with Sunny. He then met the driver at the top of the stairs and took the three large suitcases from him. As he turned back to the open door, he watched Molly Winters rush toward the airplane. He could see she had Sam by the hand, backpack hanging off the arm chain created by her grip, pulling one small suitcase behind her. They had apparently left their cold-weather gear at home, choosing instead to sprint across the tarmac to the warmth of the plane. Molly wore a baseball cap over her short-cropped blonde hair, a Cubs sweatshirt that fell off one shoulder in that sexy way that they can, jeans, and chucks. He knew he shouldn't, but God, he fantasized about that girl. Something about her called to him — her vulnerability, her strength, her honesty...he couldn't be sure. He spent a lot of time avoiding her so he wouldn't get to know her enough to go there.

She had a kid. That was that.

A no-go for him.

Hard stop.

"Hey, Kerry! Thanks for waiting for us. We've never been on your plane before. This is so cool!" She gave him a solid hug. No poke in the eye like Sunny. Maybe one in the gut...

"Welcome aboard. Our plane is your plane. Let me take something. Your hands are full." Kerry put out his hands to take a piece of luggage.

She huffed out a breath from the exertion. "Take Sam. Show him where to sit. I've got this stuff."

"Uh, ok. Hey, Sam. Come on in, buddy. You can sit anywhere you like." The kid's face lit with excitement.

"Cool! Window seat."

"Please. Window seat, please. That's what you meant, right, Sam?" Molly moved past Kerry, leaving a trail of fresh scent lingering between them. Lemon? No, not lemon but definitely something sweet and citrus.

Sunny interrupted his daydream. "Wow, the Montgomerys really are so generous. Letting the help on board with us now, are we?"

"Sunny!" Kerry chided. She was citrus too. Lime, sour...very sour.

"Hi. I'm Molly Winters." Molly smiled and held out a hand to shake, but Sunny barely looked at it, or her, before moving on. "I'm Jillian's sister..."

"Uh huh. Come, Kerry. Let's catch up...up here." She took his hand and moved them not so subtly to two seats toward the front of the plane, sliding her arm under his on the armrest between them and taking the champagne Bridget offered before takeoff. And that was that. No eighties retro book for him. Just Sunny Paulson for four hours.

Lord, give me grace.

Chapter 2

IN ALL HER TWENTY-THREE years, she had never seen anything quite that color blue, with hints of green, turquoise, and even purple. She'd seen Lake Michigan a million times, grown up next to it, and on it in her dad's boats. She'd thought it was the most beautiful of views. But this...this Caribbean blue was...overwhelming, biblical, orgasmic even.

The views of the islands' lush greenery with white-sand beaches visible from ten thousand feet left her speechless. She considered just not getting off the airplane at all. This was what she had come to see, what she had never dreamed she would see. It was enough. All things going forward would be disappointing in comparison, she was sure of it. But Sam pulled her off the plane nonetheless.

Molly observed Sunny's reaction to the same view. She didn't seem fazed in the least. Same old Saint Kitts to her. Same old tall palms. Same old charmed life.

Molly reminded herself to act cool, blend in, and stop being such a rube.

"My driver is here. Are you sure you want to go with Michael? It's so...pedestrian. He can take the others, and my guy can drop you off after we say hello to my parents. They always want to see you." Sunny appeared irritated.

How could anyone be irritated in such a place?

"No. Thanks, though. You go on ahead. Say hello to your parents for me. Maybe we'll see you at the club for tennis this week. Michael is already here now. I'll go with him and Molly."

"Fine." *Sunny Paulson does not beg.* She air-kissed him again before pointing at her driver and then her bags.

Molly waited at the base of the plane steps and watched Kerry shake hands with a tall, robust black man about his same age who had climbed out of a bright-blue van labeled "Blue Banana Tours."

"Michael, buddy. So good to see you. Thanks for coming to get us."

"Anytime, man. You know that. Hello, Miss Sunny. No air-kisses for me?" Sunny put her sunglasses on and walked past Michael without a word. "Ah, yes, that's about right. Same old Sunny." He emphasized the word "old" with a smile. "Now, who is this beautiful young lady?" Emphasis on "young" for effect, although Sunny was well out of earshot. Molly liked him already.

Kerry turned to Molly and then back to his friend. "This is Molly Winters."

"Hello, my queen. And is this your prince?" He pointed to Sam, who was holding her hand.

"Absolutely. This is Sam. So nice to meet you, Michael." She shook his hand briskly.

"Well, let's get you out to the house. I'm sure you are expected. Queen Molly, you sit right up there next to me so you don't miss a thing. Prince, second row with King Kerry here. I've got the bags."

They piled into the van for the ride across the island. The roads on Saint Kitts wound tightly and, at times, left only room for one-way traffic. Michael assured Molly, "Close your eyes, love. I got this."

She couldn't help her nervous giggle, though she didn't close her eyes. She wanted to see it all – every nook and cranny, mountain and sea, each and every mansion and shack. They appeared to be all mixed together, living in harmony. She felt a little spark of magic. As for the food, she imagined the tastes would be just as outrageous.

"How are you part of this crazy Montgomery family?" Michael asked as he pulled to the side of the road to allow another car to pass.

Molly watched as the van squeezed between the rock face and the other car's side mirror with just inches to spare. "I'm not really part of the Montgomery family. Jillian is my sister. She's married to Drew, who is my best friend from childhood. I'm really here to help out with their twins."

"Oh, yes. Kit and Kat. I brought them in a few days ago. Cutie pies, those two."

"Kit and Kat?" she asked with a confused wrinkle of her forehead. Turning back, Kerry laughed and shrugged.

"Don't you know? Kerry, you need to share with your guest. Tell me, who is our island of Saint Kitts named for?"

"That would be Saint Christopher."

Molly mumbled under her breath without turning to Kerry, "Smartypants."

"Yes, Christopher, like your nephew. We shorten it to Kit. And then there is your niece, Katherine. I shortened that one. Kit and Kat. Like the candy..." He smiled proudly.

"Ah, I know them as Chris and Katie. But I like Kit Kat better. That may stick. Get it? Stick..." She gave him a quick tap with her elbow.

Michael boomed out a laugh as Sam and Kerry let out groans from the back seat.

"Ok, my turn. How are you a part of this family, Michael?"

"Genetics, can't you see, love? Really, Kerry here invaded my island when we were just kids, maybe a little younger than your boy there. He tried to steal my girlfriend, and I popped him in the jaw. We've been friends ever since."

Kerry chimed in from the back seat: "That's not how I remember the story. I remember getting popped, but the rest is...hazy at best. Michael came by the house one day and ingratiated himself with my mother. She never made him leave, so...here we are."

"It's true." Michael laughed heartily with the others. In fact, they laughed all the way to the house.

The house...ohh, the house: stucco painted the lightest shade of yellow, wide white shutters, and surrounded by lush green bushes and tall palm trees. The thick, carved mahogany door welcomed them into the open-air first floor. Cool white marble floors contrasted with dark cabinetry. The entire first floor seemed to funnel its occupants toward the open-air living room with a vaulted white wooden ceiling, upholstered couches in creamy white with sea-foam-green pillows, and two huge cool-blue pots with arching plants reaching toward a view like she had never seen. The infinity pool fell into a few hundred yards of rolling green space before the turquoise of the sea took over, stretching to the horizon.

"Mama, can I swim? Please, please, please?" Sam was tugging her hand toward the pool.

"I can't take my eyes off of it. I've never seen the ocean. Or is it the Caribbean Sea?"

Kerry stepped up behind her and rested a hand on her shoulder. She thought it might have been the only thing keeping her from floating away. "That is the Caribbean Sea."

"And there isn't a single cloud in that sky."

"Rainy season ends in November. We might not see a cloud all weekend."

She turned to look up at his profile. "Does it ever get old? The sunshine or that view?"

"Never." His hand glided across her back gently as he moved away. She felt an unfamiliar tug inside but ignored it...sort of.

"Mom! Can I swim?" Sam was impatiently waiting for her to join him at the edge of the pool.

"Not yet, buddy. We've got to get our suitcase upstairs and find your swim trunks and your lifejacket." She squatted down to his level. "Remember, we are guests here, bud. We use please and thank you..."

Sam interrupted her as he already knew what she was going to say. "Grace and grateful… I know, Mom. You don't have to tell me all the time. I got this." She laughed at his impression of Michael, but she also felt a twinge of sadness. He was growing up faster than she could keep up with the feelings that surrounded time passing. She knew she couldn't freeze time, but she sure wished for that superpower some days – the ones that held her happiness and his youthful innocence.

"Ok, you got this. Now, move it or lose it. Let's go find the babies and have some fun."

"HEY THERE. WHY ARE you making breakfast? You're on vacation. You should be sleeping in, walking the beach, or swimming in that big blue ocean you can't stop drooling over." Kerry stepped into the living room and wandered toward the kitchen space. "It's not even seven A.M."

Molly dropped the oil on the hot griddle, making it sizzle. One of her favorite sounds. "Sleeping in? What's that? I've been up for hours."

"You know what I mean. You should be relaxing, not working."

"This is relaxing. Cooking is fun for me. I'm making food for the family and playing with this amazing range. It's definitely an upgrade from my apartment stove. Plus, I'm a terrible sleeper anyway."

Kerry settled onto a barstool on the opposite side of the big quartz kitchen island. When she used the griddle, she faced him directly. Even in his white t-shirt and pajama pants, he looked like he was ready to run a board meeting. His hair was mussed, though. She liked that. And she wasn't going to complain about the biceps pushing out of the t-shirt either. "Me too. Sometimes, my insomnia feels like a curse. But not today. What are you making? It smells great."

"I wanted to do something for CJ since he invited me along to this tropical paradise. It's his Turkish delight."

"Excuse me? It's his what now?" Kerry appeared genuinely lost.

She laughed easily at his confusion. "It's a silly game Sam and I play. We try to guess someone's all-time favorite food. You know, the food you would choose as your last meal on death row or eat every day on your deserted island. You'd give up Narnia for it. You know...Turkish delight."

"Oh, I love C.S. Lewis. And CJ goes for pancakes?"

"Not just pancakes. My cinnamon latte pancakes." She scooped a generous amount of batter onto the griddle.

"How do you know that this is his Turkish delight?" He put up air quotes around the phrase, and she flushed with embarrassment over the childishness of the game.

"I've made these for him more times than I can count. They were his hangover breakfast when he used to crash at Drew's townhouse after a night of debauchery. Before Hailey, that is. When I think of CJ, I think both sweet and lush. Each meal kind of matches the person. That's part of the game."

"I have never understood why women think CJ is sweet. Then again, I have never understood women, so that might be the root of the issue."

"Aww, are you jealous?"

"Of CJ? Never, but I can't believe that bastard has been getting his own private Turkish delight every time he drinks too much. You are too nice to him, Molly. Ok. I'll play. What's my delight?"

"I'm sure I don't know." Between the heat of the range and her own embarrassment over the childishness of the game, her cheeks must have been lit up like a Christmas tree. She turned back to put the bowls in the sink and gain a little composure. "You don't have to play this with me. It's ridiculous, I know."

"No, I like it." He looked at her from across the kitchen island. "But you think I'm a snob. You think I wouldn't play a silly game for fun. Right?"

"I didn't say that. And I wouldn't. I don't know you well enough to guess your delight, that's all." She started flipping the pancakes when she saw the batter bubbles reach the top.

Kerry looked down at his clasped hands. "Why is that?"

"Why is what?"

"Why do you spend time with both of my younger brothers but not with me?"

Oh, what fresh hell is this? "I've...I've never had the opportunity, I guess. You didn't hang out in my dad's boat shop, like Drew. He and I were just...always together. He probably remembers it differently. I'm sure he thought I was the pesky little sister he couldn't get rid of. Probably still trying." She nodded her head, more to herself than him.

"Fair enough. You should know his delight, then?"

"Oh yeah, he's easy."

"Always has been..." He laughed at his own joke. She thought she hadn't seen him smile that easily, that relaxed, in a few years.

"White cheddar mac n' cheese with bacon and sweet peas. Total comfort food, with a little soul from the bacon and a little sweet from the peas." She shrugged.

"Huh. This could be fun." Standing, he took one of the strawberry slices she had cut for breakfast and popped it into his mouth, moving smoothly toward the living room. "Let me know when you figure me out."

Molly grinned to herself. She had an inkling that would be a bit more of a challenge. She knew Kerry was kind, quiet, family-oriented. Hell, she'd spent most of her childhood Christmases or Fourth of Julys with his family, with him even, but he was still a bit of an enigma to her. He had been so sympathetic when her father had passed away, especially given the shameful circumstances of his death. He never made her feel like it was her fault for not knowing her father's ulterior motive, for not knowing he would want to hurt Jillian. He'd made her feel...forgiven. She remembered that in particular, even though those first days after Jillian's injury, and her dad's death, were still a bit of a blur.

On the other hand, Kerry was a powerful man with a weighty and complicated job in the ship-building industry, working with his father, JP Montgomery. She would never have thought him a snob, but he wasn't playful like CJ either. He was...serious, with slightly sad eyes and a bit of a tortured nature. She was a sucker for weary eyes and a wounded soul... *Crap!*

"What are you grinning about, and why are you working so hard?" Hailey popped down the stairs with her usual grace and the pumped spirit of a happy woman about to marry the man of her dreams. She tamed her auburn curls back into a ponytail as she headed into the kitchen. Molly had always admired Hailey's style, even looked up to her when Hailey was a teenager. She had a casual sophistication about her, and she was still confident and open-hearted even though life hadn't been particularly easy on her. These days, their kids got along well too. Molly thought Sam had a crush on Hailey's six-year-old daughter, Natalie. How could she tell? Sam never liked being ordered around unless Natalie was the one doing the ordering.

"I'm just making breakfast."

CJ swaggered in behind the range island in swim trunks, a Blackhawks t-shirt, and bare feet. He couldn't have looked more relaxed. He whispered, "Are those what I think they are?" pointing at the pancakes.

"Maybe. You'll have to taste them to find out. Everyone can try them. Breakfast is ready. I've got pancakes, bacon, fresh-cut fruit, and orange juice."

Hailey walked around to the small beverage fridge under the island. "There is some good champagne in here. How about we make it mimosas with breakfast?"

CJ put his hands on Molly's shoulders and leaned in close to her ear, but he still spoke loud enough for the others to hear. "Do you want to run away with me to a tropical island?" He smiled at Hailey as he asked.

"Why, CJ Montgomery, your fiancé is right there."

Hailey laughed. "It's ok, Molly. I'll marry you too if you'll make these pancakes for me. They are magical." She sat at the dining table, exuding sounds of delight.

Kerry made himself a plate. "They can't be that good..." He took a bite. "Oh...never mind. They are." Molly heard him groan out a sound she believed was intended to convey enjoyment.

"Well, what are you all going to do today?" she asked, attempting to change the subject from her cooking to vacation practicalities.

CJ spoke first. "I thought we might try paddle boarding. Hailey hasn't done it before, and the kids will enjoy it. It's pretty easy. Even Drew can do it." She watched Kerry laugh easily with his brother. CJ took another helping of pancakes.

"Sam would love that. Is it ok if he goes too? I can stay here with the twins."

"No way. You and Sam are both coming along. Mom is on twin duty today, and she is going to love every minute of it. You can't take that away from her. I thought we'd try Cockleshell Bay. How's your knowledge of reggae music?"

"Umm..." Before she could finish her answer, they all heard the dulcet tones of Sunny Paulson announcing her own arrival.

She pushed the big front door open, sauntered over to the dining table, and leaned in to air-kiss Kerry's cheeks. "Ahhh, hello, Kerry love...and CJ." She waved her sunglasses vaguely in his direction. She didn't acknowledge either of the other women in the room, including the one who was to be the bride.

CJ sat back from the table. "Hello, Sunny," he answered with a sigh. "You know the wedding isn't until Saturday. You're early."

She waved off his tone as if she thought herself welcome to see the Queen of England if it fit her own calendar. "Yes, well, I came to see if

Kerry wanted to play tennis at the club this morning. We always play when he is on the island." She sat on an empty dining chair and looked directly at Molly. "Are you having mimosas? I'll have one with orange and pomegranate, just a twist of lime too."

Molly watched CJ stifle a grin. She said deliberately, "I'll see what we have."

Kerry objected. "No, Molly. You are not here to serve anyone, least of all Sunny. I'll get it."

"What? Kerry dear, let her help. She wants to help. And you need to get dressed if we are going to play before it gets too hot. I hate it when it gets too hot."

Kerry gave Molly an unenthusiastic look before they both stood and headed toward the kitchen. He whispered to her before turning off toward the stairs. "Her delight? Human flesh, with a twist of lime."

Molly giggled while she poured the Champagne.

Chapter 3

CJ PULLED THE SUV INTO the Water Sports parking area above the beach. The morning breeze ruffled Molly's purple tie-dyed cover-up as she jumped out of the passenger's side. She pushed her sunglasses up onto her blonde cap of hair and took in the moment. She was on vacation in a tropical paradise with her son and sister.

She made a mental note to pick up some fresh seafood at the market she saw on the way so she could at least try to pay back the Montgomerys for their hospitality. Maybe lobster was Kerry's delight? Why was she thinking about him all of a sudden? He was off at the tennis club with Sunny, doing millionaire-y things with other millionaire-y people. She gave herself a little shake and opened the back door of the SUV. Sam, little Natalie, Hailey, Drew, and Jillian climbed out like it was some kind of clown car. *These are my monkeys.*

Hailey announced, "I'm going to get one of the cabanas rented for us. Molly, why don't you come with me?"

"Sure. I'll help you carry the beach bags. Sam, stay with Drew. And make sure he puts on his life jacket. And sunscreen." She turned back to Hailey. "Maybe I should go with the boys. Sam's not a strong swimmer."

"They'll be fine. He's got Drew, right? Come on."

"Ok. You're right. Let's get a spot to land." Reggae music played from the small shack called a bar set up at the end of the beach. Individual cabanas with what looked like queen-sized outdoor four-poster beds under lazy white canopies spotted the beach sand. Looking through them, she could see the island of Nevis in the distance and blue-green blotches forming a patchwork quilt of water in between.

A few minutes later, Hailey returned from the makeshift beach stand across the sidewalk. "I got this one here. We're going to need the shade before too long. I don't want any weird tan lines peeking out under my wedding dress."

"Ooh, now you're talking my language. What does your dress look like?" They walked together over the warming sand.

"I found it in a sweet little shop in North Carolina. I went back to close the sale on the house there and move everything officially to CJ's loft in Chicago. I wasn't planning on shopping there, but I had a free afternoon and just sort of wandered in. Their selection was pretty small, but it only takes one, right?"

"Those are the best finds. When you're not really looking. Sort of feels like the dress found you."

Hailey set all the beach bags in the cabana and fell back onto the mattress, her auburn curls spreading above her. "Ahhh... I love this place. I love CJ. I love my daughter. Can you tell I'm a little over the top this week? Just slap me if I get out of control."

"Over the top is totally appropriate for the bride. Wouldn't be right any other way."

Jillian joined the women at the cabana with three margaritas, a lime twist in each plastic cup. Molly thought of Kerry playing tennis with sour-faced Sunny Paulson and took a hearty sip.

Feeling emboldened by the cool liquid, she engaged in a rare moment of girl talk. "Ok, the dress, then..."

"Right. It is the prettiest silver-pink lace with this deep V in the front, sleeveless. It has this thin satin belt across the waist and a flowing A-line skirt to just above the sand. Now that I think of it, I should not have had your pancakes for breakfast." Hailey ran a hand across her stomach. "I'll just have this margarita for lunch."

The women laughed together, soon-to-be sisters in different ways. Molly and Jillian were half-sisters through their mom, and Jillian and Hailey would soon be sisters-in-law through marriage. For a split second, Molly actually saw herself belong in this family. *Hold the phone, sister. You aren't a Montgomery and never will be.*

"Mom! Mom! Look at me! I'm on the paddleboard! I'm doing it!" Sam's calls pulled her out of the wayward thoughts. He was standing on a six-foot board with an oar equally long in his hands, pushing himself through the calm waters of the Caribbean. Natalie was kneeling on another one not too far away. She had CJ standing in the water next to her while Drew helped Sam. Molly waved, acknowledging him before he yelled again.

"Great job, honey!"

When she turned back, Jillian and Hailey were lying in the sun with the straps of their bathing suits untied. Hailey covered her eyes to see Molly better. "You could go join them. You know you want to."

"No. I really want to... No. I can stay here with you guys."

"What? You really want to what?" Jillian levered up onto her elbows and raised her sunglasses to look at her sister.

"I want to take a long walk, no, a stroll down the beach. Like you always see in the movies. Leave the world behind...just me and my thoughts. Now I'm the one being dramatic."

"Well, then go. The men have their eyes on the kids. We'll keep our eyes on the men. It's ok to go."

"Ok, but I'll just wander this way a bit and then come back." She wasn't sure why she felt like she had to ask permission.

"Take your time. Stroll to your heart's content. You're on vacation."

"You might need to tattoo that on my butt before it really sinks in. I'm loving it here, but relaxation is not one of my top three skills." She pulled her cover-up off and stuffed it in the beach bag, slipped out of her flip-flops, and headed off down the beach.

"She needs to de-stress. We've got to find her a guy, pronto." Jillian flopped back onto the soft mattress.

"Yep!" said Hailey.

"I heard that!" Molly laughed and spun in a small circle. *I'm on vacation.*

She'd never had so much fun in all her life, and it had only been twenty-four hours since she'd left cold, snowy Chicago. She really never let herself have fun, if she were being honest. Never one to see herself as the victim, she had preferred to be seen as self-sufficient since she'd been a child. She thought it one of her best qualities. She had certainly needed it after her mom had died. And after she had gotten pregnant at sixteen. Her dad had helped after Sam's arrival. But she'd lost him too. The only person she had ever relied on was Drew, and he'd run off and married her sister. Not that she minded. She was thrilled to see them happy. Her own wants – and needs, such as they were – had been back-burner stuff since Sam had arrived. She would do anything for that kid, but it didn't mean life was always a ton of fun. Today, though...today was a good day.

Lost in thought, she almost ran into Kerry while looking down at the sand squishing between her toes and daydreaming of lives gone un-lived, of what ifs and what might have beens.

"Hey. Earth to Molly. What were you thinking about?"

"Oh, hey. You know, thinking through life's great existential crises. Personal development, yada yada yada..." Her sentence trailed off when she looked up to take him in. He wore only swimming trunks and aviator sunglasses. His bare chest was chiseled, no doubt, but not overly puffed up like some of those bodybuilders', and he had the slightest hint of chest hair spreading out toward his broad shoulders. His skin ran smoothly over the ripples of his abdomen and down to the V at his shorts. *Whoa.* She needed to jump in the water to cool herself down.

"Okay... When you've sorted out the mysteries of life, want to learn how to paddle board?" Kerry smiled brightly as he wrapped an arm around her shoulder and turned to walk in her direction.

"When did you get here, by the way? I thought you were playing tennis."

"I was. I did."

"Did you bring Sunny back to the beach with you?"

Kerry let loose a genuine chuckle. "Cockleshell Bay is not exactly Sunny Paulson territory."

"Really? It just became my very favorite place in the whole world." She looked down before continuing. "Sorry. Do you like her? Wait, don't answer that. You don't have to answer that. I shouldn't have asked that."

"It's no problem. I know how she seems. Sunny is...complicated. She's not really as mean as she acts sometimes. She's...appropriate, I guess."

"Wow! Will they write that on her tombstone? Here lies Sunny Paulson. She was...appropriate."

He shook his head. "That's not what I mean. My parents like her. Well, my parents like her parents. My peers expect someone like her."

She nodded. "Also a glowing recommendation."

He bent down, breaking the connection between them. He picked up a rock and tossed it into the Caribbean. "I'm not saying this right. I don't want to be with Sunny any more than you want to be with...me. I'd guess. But I'm the oldest. Always been the responsible one, which isn't hard with CJ just behind me. There are expectations for me that the others don't feel. Or maybe they just shove them off better than I do."

"So, let me get this straight. CJ can marry Hailey for love, and Drew can marry my sister for love, but poor Kerry must marry for status, money, or appropriateness?"

"Who said I was getting married? I haven't even found my Turkish delight yet. How can I be expected to have found the love of my life if I don't even know what food I'd give up Narnia for?"

Molly laughed at him. She didn't feel like he was mocking her game as much as himself. "The love of your life, eh? There's a romantic in there somewhere."

"Never said there wasn't. Now, do you want to learn to paddle board before we head back to the house or not?"

"Umm...yes. I think I would." He took her hand and pulled her toward the water's edge where Drew, CJ, Sam, and Natalie had abandoned their boards, apparently in search of beer and ice cream respectively.

"Ok." She slapped her hands to her thighs. "What do I do?" She picked the heavy board up out of the sand.

"I'm impressed already. We put the board in the shallower water here. I'll walk out with you until you get the hang of it. I can hold the board steady while you sit on your knees." She did as he instructed. "Ok, now, push up to a stand and get your balance. Then you use the oar to push yourself forward."

The board wobbled, and she overcompensated, causing her to fall off the right side. Popping back up out of the water, she couldn't help but laugh. "Ahhh! The kids made it look so easy."

"It's ok. Let's try again. I'll help you back on." Kerry put his hands on her waist, just where the straps of her bikini crossed her hips. Her back rested against his flat chest. She felt him hesitate for just a moment, probably judging whether he could lift her or not. "Ready? One. Two. Three." She jumped to help him lift her out of the waist-deep water. His strength plus her jump meant she slid over the board and splashed into the water on the other side. She popped back up out of the water to find him laughing at her.

"Why did you jump?"

"I didn't think you could lift me up."

"Oh my God. Who do I look like? CJ? Come back around." Instead of walking around the board to try again, she dove under it and took him down at the ankles. They wrestled under the water for a moment before they both broke the surface. Kerry's laughter was infectious. She couldn't help but join in. He grabbed her wrist and pulled her in closer. They both stopped laughing.

She felt a pressure build in her chest, one she hadn't experienced in a very long time. The space between them suddenly felt too small given the expanse of the sea in which they stood, or maybe it was the expanse of the differences between them. She would process that later. For now, she needed to get back on the board before he did something he might regret with someone not quite appropriate.

"Kerry..." She looked at his wet chest with just a hint of blonde hair at the center.

"Yes..." He looked at her directly, gently pushing a wayward strand of hair off of her forehead.

"You're..."

"Yes..."

"You're standing on my foot."

"Oh God, sorry." He pushed back, relieving the pressure with space between them, and let her climb on the board herself.

Thirty minutes later, she was standing up on the board, moving through the water with Kerry navigating his own board behind her.

"Mom! You're doing it! Good job!" Sam yelled from the shoreline, a dripping ice cream cone in his hand.

She waved back to him.

"Molly, come back to the house with Kerry. We're heading back. We'll take Sam with us and leave your bag in the cabana," Drew yelled, standing next to Sam on the beach.

"Oh, I can come back with you. Wait a minute. I'll come in."

Drew waved her off. "Stay, have fun. We'll meet you back at the house."

Feeling like she couldn't argue from the paddle board without risking her balance, she sent up a thumbs up sign to Drew.

"Do you want to go in now?" Kerry offered from behind her.

"No, no. Let's go a little further. He's fine with Drew. Besides, I'm having fun."

"Great. Me too."

WHAT WAS I THINKING? He'd rushed back from the club to meet them all at the beach because he'd wanted to be with his family. He would regret dropping Sunny off in such a hurry the next time he saw her. She would make him regret it. What was he thinking? He was thinking about Molly Winters, about her small, tight little body in a bright-blue strapless bikini. He was thinking about seeing her relaxed and easy. He was not thinking about Sam, her son, a kid about the same age as Bettina.

He didn't hold anything against Sam. Kerry found him to be a great kid – polite, funny, playful. But it didn't change what had happened in Kerry's past and his post-traumatic need to avoid ever having any kids of his own. That was the word his child therapist had used back at sixteen when Bettina had died. Post-traumatic must be clinical speak for regret or pain, or maybe soul-crushing guilt. Whatever the word, he'd sworn never to have kids of his own or be with someone who wanted them. That made Sunny even more appropriate. She wouldn't touch a kid with a ten-foot pole, let alone carry one for nine months. She was safe.

"What'cha drinking?" Molly interrupted his thoughts, joining him at the table in the bar, now dressed in a simple pale-blue sundress and flip-flops. She had brushed her wet hair back quickly, and it now fell to the side loosely, making her pretty eyes larger, and bluer somehow.

"Skol. It's a local island beer. Want one?" Kerry started to rise to get her a drink from the bar.

"No, no. Sit down. Relax. I can get it. Be right back." She pushed off from the chair and waved him back down.

Kerry watched her walk toward the bar and forgot to look away. He had nothing but respect for Molly – small and mighty, hardworking, genuine, and apparently a spectacular cook. He had enjoyed spending the last day with her, more consecutive time than they'd ever spent in the past despite her being akin to a sister to Drew.

She leaned forward onto her elbows and laughed with the bartender over something Kerry couldn't hear. She hadn't had much laughter in her life. He remembered when her mom had died. He'd been just a kid himself, easily distracted from the pain she must have been feeling. She hadn't come around as much after she'd gotten pregnant with Sam. Kerry had been off in college by that time anyway. No, he'd been in grad school. *Damn, I am old.*

She'd only come in and out of his life at holidays for a good ten years. He'd been there, though, when her dad had died a couple of years ago. Kerry had stayed with her at the hospital until Jillian had woken up. What a terrible time for her. He'd seen her devastation then, paid attention to her pain, pushed down any feelings he might have allowed to blossom under different circumstances. *Probably time to do that again.*

"Yum. This place looks amazing. It's so much bigger than it looked from the beach. I want to come back for food sometime." Molly sat in the chair across from him and smiled.

"Let's have dinner." It just sort of came out. *Not the plan, man.*

"You don't want to head back to the house? Have dinner with your family?" She gestured with the bottle and then took a sip.

"They can fend for themselves. The cook here makes some mean fritters. And the lobster is pretty great too. My mom and the rest of them will watch Sam. We can call if you'd feel better about it." Kerry started to pull out his cell phone.

"No." She put up a hand to stop him from producing the phone. "I'm on vacation. That's what I'm supposed to say according to Jilly and Hailey. Sam's in good hands. Let's eat and explore a little. I saw a fresh seafood market on the way in that I would love to stop at on the way home if it's still open. Your parents have been so generous to let me come along. I'd like to say thank you."

"Sounds perfect. But you don't need to work for your vacation. They see you as family, you know. Not that I would be discouraging you from cooking. For purely unselfish reasons, of course. Where did you learn to cook?"

"Here and there, I guess. It's always been an escape for me. Times get tough, I know I can always go to the kitchen. Experiment with something new and forget about reality."

"Why didn't you go to culinary school, then?" He sipped his beer.

"That pesky reality again. And Sam."

"Right." *Sam is her reality.*

"I probably couldn't have gone even if I didn't have him. It can be pretty competitive. I'm just a home cook."

"Now, that's just not true. You could do anything you put your mind to. Still could."

"I've done some junior college classes. Took some business courses so I could open the catering business without losing my shirt."

Heaven help me. "How is the business?" His voice was an octave too high. He tried to clear his throat, as if it would clear his thoughts.

"Decent. I'll never be the one doing fancy society weddings or anything. Just small catered meals for private events. It seems to be the right fit for me."

"I don't think you are giving yourself enough credit."

"I don't know. Sometimes, when you change a hobby into a career, the magic gets lost."

"So wise for one so young." He smiled. "Where do you come up with the recipes?"

"Sometimes, the event has specific desires. Sometimes, I get to play a bit with my cookbooks or from online sources. Often, I try out new stuff on my shelter guys. They always give me honest feedback."

"Shelter guys? You mean homeless men? In the city?"

"Yes. They need to eat too. There is a shelter a few blocks from our apartment. I drop off extras from events a lot. The guys know me now. I can empathize with a lot of their situations."

"Saint Molly." He picked up his menu to see what was on special that they might try while his gut worried for her safety more than he cared to admit.

Molly laughed. "Umm...pregnant at sixteen, dad turned out to have a pretty malicious agenda. I've got some broken halos, friend. Saint has never been part of any nickname."

"It should be. I hope you are being safe with these men. Not everyone is as nice as you."

"Yes, Dad."

Ouch. "Well then, what should we eat?"

"I want to try the fritters and the fresh fruit salad with the poppy seed dressing."

"Ok. I'm getting the crab...and some of your fritters." Kerry got up to order at the bar. He brought back two more beers and set them on their table. "Look at that sunset."

"I know. And the breeze is heaven after the day in the sun. I had a really great time with you today, Kerry."

"The night is young, Saint Molly. The night is young."

The food was nothing short of amazing. Watching Molly devour it was even better. She talked her way back into the kitchen to swap stories with the chef.

"He's a native. Nice guy. He knows Michael."

"I suspect everyone on this island knows Michael."

"Well, seems like he likes him. He is going to email me his fritters recipe."

"Does everyone who meets you fall in love with you just a little bit?"

She didn't appear embarrassed at his question, just brushed it off with her usual grace. "I don't think so. The circle of people who love me is pretty small, but I'll let you know if he professes his undying love...right after I get the recipe."

They stopped at the seafood market on the way home. He wanted to hold her hand as they strolled but thought better of it. Just the magic of Saint Kitts getting to him.

After stashing the goods in the cooler, they walked a little farther up the street to the restaurant and nightclub area. Molly stopped at every menu plastered on the stucco to see what delights each might hold. She glowed from the day of sun and from her interest in the local food and culture. Kerry watched her stop and talk to one of the chefs working a food counter across the street. He dipped into the closest shop before walking across to meet her.

"Here. You might want to wrap this around your shoulders. It's cooling off." He handed her a soft wrap patterned in blue and white flowers.

"Thank you for this. You read my mind." She placed it over her shoulders and tied it in the front.

"Find your delight yet?"

"No, but I thought I might come back here tomorrow if I can get away and sample a few things."

"You can try to escape from my mother's agenda, but I wouldn't recommend it. I believe tomorrow is slated for bachelor- and bachelorette-type things. Given the size of Saint Kitts, though, you'll probably end up here anyway."

"Oh, but I'm not in the wedding party. I can come back on my own after they go out."

"I'd clear that with my mother first. She likely has plans. She always does."

"Ok. I'll talk to her." They walked slowly, without touching, taking in the sights and sounds of the marketplace, inhaling the scents from the restaurants, capturing the culture of the island that he loved. "What are the boys doing for the bachelor party?"

"I'm not at liberty to share Montgomery men's night secrets."

She slapped him gently on the chest. "I've often wondered about those evenings."

"Loose lips sink ships. And I'm not in the business of sinking ships. Ready to head home?"

"Never, but I'd like to check on Sam."

They wandered back to the car, and Kerry drove, mostly in silence. It was too dark to see much of the island, or he would have offered a tour. He found that he was enjoying her company more than her pancakes this morning, especially that they could be quiet together without it feeling awkward. He parked the car in the driveway and walked her to the stairway leading to the bedrooms.

"Aren't you going up to bed?" She looked so pretty with the moonlight behind her.

"Not quite yet. Insomnia will take over if I don't wind down a bit before I head up. I really enjoyed spending the day with you, Molly."

"Me too. You're not who I expected, Kerry Montgomery. Not who I expected at all. Goodnight. I hope you get some sleep." She leaned in and kissed his cheek before turning to dash up the stairs.

Sleep was a long way off...

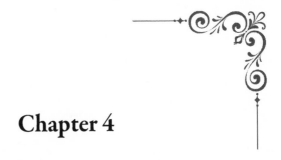

Chapter 4

MOLLY PULLED CINNAMON rolls out of the oven and slowly waved the scent toward Kerry, who was sleeping on the couch in the open-air living room. Laughter echoed in from the deck outside. She watched as the scent entered his dream and rolled him toward awakening. He rubbed his hands over his face and then through his mop of hair, which was still salty from yesterday's adventure in the sea.

"Kerry, son. There are six bedrooms in this house. Why are you sleeping on that couch?" Andrea poured him some coffee while she chided her oldest son, but she carried the cup over to him anyway.

"Good morning to you too, Mom. Thanks." He took a sip from the steaming mug.

Andrea turned to Molly. "If I slept on that couch, I wouldn't walk for a week afterwards."

She shrugged. "I'm a mom of a young child. I can sleep anywhere, anytime – just never for very long."

"I remember those days. Don't roll your eyes when I tell you that you'll miss them. Oh, I love that you are all here. I love having kids in this house again. Kerry, remember that year we had your birthday party here? Which one was that? Fifteen? So many kids. That was fun."

"Wow! That's not your average birthday party at the Chuck E. Cheese. Local kids or Chicago kids?" Molly poured some orange juice in the glass to her right, hoping Kerry would join them at the table.

"Mostly local. You met Michael. He and Kerry go way back. And some cousins from home. That was the year before Bettina. She was here. Remember, Kerry?"

Kerry stood and walked to the dining table. He kissed the top of his mom's head and continued on past her to the stairs. "I remember, Mom."

"Want some cinnamon rolls? Or eggs and sausage?" Molly said up into the air, but then she looked after him when he walked past.

"Thanks, no. I think I'll skip breakfast and go for a run. I'll be back later."

"Wow, he's grouchy this morning." Molly picked up Andrea's plate and carried it with her own to the kitchen to serve the warm rolls.

"It's my fault. I shouldn't have mentioned Bettina. I know better."

"Who is she, and why can't we mention her?"

"Bettina is my niece, my brother Jack's daughter. She was such a little spirit. A lot like Natalie out there." Andrea pointed toward the deck, where CJ and Natalie were playing a card game and rolling in laughter, completely enthralled with each other.

"What happened?" The two women sat together at the table.

"She drowned."

"Oh!" Molly covered her mouth with her hand, not meaning to let the shocked sound escape as quickly as it had.

"It was so long ago, but it feels like yesterday. We were at the house in Chicago. She and Kerry went out on the powerboat together. He was sixteen. She was five. She was so spunky – cheering him to go faster from the rear of the boat. He was looking forward, pushing the accelerator lever. She fell off the back." Molly reached out to hold Andrea's hand. "They were kids. No one was wearing a life jacket. Kerry didn't hear her fall because of the noise of the boat. As soon as he figured out that she was gone, he circled back, but he couldn't find her."

"Oh, that is awful. I can't imagine the panic he must have felt. But he can't blame himself. Can he? He was just a kid."

"Tell that to him. I tried to convince him of that. His dad tried. The best therapists in the city tried."

"Did they ever find her?"

"Kerry trolled that lake for hours, hoping she'd found a branch or a raft to hang onto until someone could get to her. He dove in the water where he thought she must have been, but Lake Michigan is so deep and the water can be so choppy. He's lucky he didn't drown. The state police sent out the divers. They found her a few days later."

Molly rubbed Andrea's back gently. She started to speak but thought she might overstep her bounds. "It... Never mind."

"What were you going to say? It's ok."

"It changed him, the experience of it, the panic and the anxiety. I know how that feels. Now he's the responsible one. The stand-up guy to CJ's clown. Something like that would change a person for sure."

"I miss the carefree boy he always was before that day. He loved Bettina like a little sister."

Molly pushed her plate forward, not sure she could eat anything now. She rested her chin on her open hand. "I must have been about her age when it happened. I don't remember hearing about it, but who remembers much from age five. And then I lost my mom. That time is a blur for me. I'm sorry it happened to her, and to him."

"Me too. I shouldn't have brought it up."

"It's part of your family's story. You shouldn't have to forget her."

"But I shouldn't have ruined his memory of this place. He loves being here more than just about anywhere. I think he gets to forget that it ever happened when he's here. Ok." Andrea patted at her wet cheeks, gently drying her loose tears. "Enough sad tears for today. We have a wedding tomorrow. I'll be puffy in the pictures, so only happy stuff for the rest of the day."

"On it. Where are you all headed today?"

"You all? Oh, honey, you are coming along on this ride. We have a spa day planned first over at the club. Hailey's parents and Amy get in

37

later this morning. They are staying nearby at the Marriott, and Hailey will stay there tonight too so there's no funny business before the wedding tomorrow."

"Funny business?" Molly stifled a laugh. "You really think they haven't done funny business before now?"

"Oh, I know my boys. They can be all about funny business, but it's not happening tonight. Not on Mama's watch."

"What's the plan for this evening? Can I make dinner before we go anywhere? I got some local seafood last night that I would love to do."

"Sounds perfect. We'll shoot for six-ish. I figure Hailey never got the bachelorette experience the first time around, so we'll send you younger ones out after dinner for a little of that too. Ms. Anna is here to stay with us and the kids tonight, so don't worry about Sam."

"Hailey and Jillian keep telling me that my mantra is 'I'm on vacation. I'm on vacation,' so I'm trying. Thank you so much for inviting me to stay with the family. I know that you included me to help with the kids, and I've done so little..."

"You stop right there, young lady. This was no pity invite. You are part of this family whether you want to be or not. You don't have to earn a spot at this table." She tapped gently on the white oak table. "Not with childcare duties or meal prep or anything else." Andrea leaned in. "Families are made a million different ways. Birth, death, marriage, friendship, love... Love changes everything in this life. Now, how about we get ourselves off to the spa. The boys can clean up the dishes."

"Well, that might just be my favorite part of the whole day." Molly smiled at Andrea, pushing down the tears that threatened. Only happy stuff...

KERRY HUSTLED UP THE stairs toward the bedroom Drew, Jillian, and the twins were using for the week. He poked his head in through the door. "Football game starting in five."

"SHHHH!" Drew jumped up out of the rocking chair and pushed Kerry's head back into the hallway.

"Hey!" Kerry pushed back hard, almost causing Drew to fall through the door into the room, but he caught himself on the door-jamb. Drew held himself perfectly still until he was sure of his balance. Then he stood and tried to close the bedroom door without making the knob click.

"What part of shush don't you understand? The twins are finally asleep. If you wake them up from their nap, I swear to God I'll beat the ever-living shit out of you right here in this hallway." Drew sank back against the wall.

"Damn, man..."

Drew held up a finger to silence him. He turned his head quickly, like a dog scenting a squirrel, before he finally exhaled. "I don't hear them. They're still asleep...lucky bastard."

Kerry whispered, "Sleep deprivation does not look good on you, brother. The girls went to do whatever it is that they do at the spa."

"I know that. That's why I'm stuck up here watching the children."

"Looked to me like you were watching the inside of your eyelids."

"Yes, well, why did you wake me up, then?"

"Football game in five."

"I can't go play football. I have to be here when these monsters wake up." He jacked his thumb back over his shoulder, toward the door to the bedroom.

"Just bring that walkie-talkie thing. Can't you sing your lullaby through it if they wake up? We're only going out on the back lawn."

"It's not a walkie-talkie, dufus. It only goes one way. I can hear them, but they can't hear me."

"Even better. We'll just strap it to your belt and get a game in. Or are you gonna use them as an excuse? What was the score the last time we all played? Oh, right. Forty-eight to six, and that was because Dad ran backwards and scored for you."

"Shut up. I'll play. And I'll kick your ass."

Kerry started down the stairs. "See you out there, Lullaby." He turned to yell it back toward Drew but had second thoughts. If he woke the kids, there'd be no game, and he was in the mood to beat his little brothers.

CJ, their dad, Natalie, and Sam waited on the back lawn, tossing the football casually and laughing. "Lullaby's coming down. But he won't play unless we listen for the small people upstairs."

Natalie chimed in: "I'm gonna be the cheerleader, but I can listen with the monitor."

Drew joined them and handed the small plastic speaker over to Nat. "Thanks, kid. Just holler if they wake up, and I'll go fix them."

Kerry muttered to CJ, "I'd like to see that." He slapped his hand on the side of the football. "Great. What are the teams?"

CJ answered back, "I'll take Lullaby. You take Dad."

Drew groaned. "Glad that nickname is sticking."

"What about me?" Sam held out his hands. "I can play."

CJ rested a hand on Sam's shoulder. "You can be with Dad and Kerry. They're gonna need you."

"Enough trash talking. What are the stakes?" Traditionally, the losing team had to buy the beer after the game, but with the kid involved, they'd need something else.

"Losers do this morning's dishes, which were tasked to us as the women left."

Kerry had pulled his dad and Sam to the side in a huddle while CJ thought through the wager. He shouted out of the group, "Deal." He turned back. "Now, Sam, what are your skills, kid?"

Sam answered quickly, "I can throw."

"Quarterback, then. Dad, you're the O line. Keep Drew off him and give Sam some time to throw. I'll go be the receiver." Kerry was impressed with Sam's confidence. He'd wait to see what the kid could do.

He would be better than Kerry's dad by leaps and bounds if all he knew was the right direction to throw the ball.

The midday sun warmed the grass under his bare feet. The tall palms gave shade to the end zones they'd marked with towels from the pool. Natalie sat on the deck railing, cheering for both sides indiscriminately. He relaxed into the ease of the game with his family despite the presence of the kids and their collective responsibility to keep them safe.

And Sam actually could throw. He'd completed a touchdown pass to Kerry on their first drive. Then CJ ran one right past Sam for six points. Defense wasn't his strong suit, but the kid was at a hundred-pound and two-foot deficit against the man.

Drew chimed in: "Better find your rubber gloves. Looks like dish-washing is in your future."

"Shut it, Lullaby. This isn't over," Kerry said while gathering for a huddle. "Listen, we don't have much time before those babies end this game. We score on this drive, and we can get a beer while they do the dirty work. Not you, Sam. You get a root beer." They laughed in the huddle together. "I'll go long. You send it as far as you can, Sam. Dad, don't hike it over his head this time. Lullaby on three. One, two, three. Lullaby!" They broke the huddle with the taunt and stepped up to the line.

Dropping back, Sam threw the ball as far as his little arm could, which was impressive for a seven-year-old, and Kerry used his height advantage to catch it over CJ's head in the end zone. CJ rolled over with a grunt after Kerry landed on him.

Sam's arms shot straight up in the air. "Touchdown!" He ran down the field and jumped into Kerry's arms.

"Awesome throw. High five!" Kerry put Sam on his shoulders, and they chanted together, "Touchdown, touchdown, touchdown!"

Natalie jumped off the railing to do congratulatory cartwheels in the grass. As if on cue, the monitor sent out a static-filled cry from the upper floor.

Drew threw the ball to his dad. "Well, that was *not* fun while it lasted. Gotta go change and feed."

Sam chimed in: "Don't forget to do the dishes."

"Nice." Kerry admired the kid's smack-talk skills while he dropped Sam back to the earth.

"Can I really have a root beer?"

"Yep. Let's go make some more dirty dishes for CJ and Drew to clean up. Snacks and beer all around."

He followed Sam inside, in step with his chants: "Touchdown, touchdown, touchdown..."

"YOU LOOK LESS GRUMPY. Feeling better after your run this morning?" Kerry watched Molly use quick, easy movements as she prepared the family meal.

"Yeah, I'm fine. I got a rare nap, too, after the football game. I do know I'd be grumpy if I was making a meal for thirteen on a moment's notice. Why didn't you go to culinary school again? You're a natural." He tried to stay out of her way while still snatching a cornbread muffin from the pan resting on the island.

"Watch out. Those are still hot." She motioned with the knife she was using to cut fruit.

He took a careful bite. "Mmmm... God, you can cook, woman."

Molly laughed. "Ah!" She put a hand on her abdomen. "Don't make me laugh. My abs still hurt from yesterday's paddleboard adventure. I should probably take that as a reason to hit the gym a little more often."

"How was the spa with the ladies?"

"Oh, divine. I got a pedicure, which was sorely needed, and sat in the sauna, uninterrupted, until your mother made us all get dressed and come back. I could live there without a second thought."

The picture of her in a skimpy towel, her body wet from hair to freshly painted toes was too much for him to bear. He changed the subject before he embarrassed himself. "What's for dinner?"

"Right. I've got lobster, corn on the cob, jalapeno cornbread...which you've already sampled, garlic green beans, fresh fruit salad, and secret dessert." She looked around the kitchen. "Should be enough, right?"

"Enough is relative. Enough for me, yes. Enough for the hungry masses about to invade...probably." He swiped a green bean and popped it in his mouth. "What is secret dessert?"

"If I told you, then I'd have to kill you. And I was just getting to like you, so don't ask."

He held up both hands in a sign of surrender. "Got it. Not asking again. Need help setting the table?" He picked up cloth napkins from the basket on the counter.

"Yes, that would be great. Just two kid's plates. The twins already ate and are playing in the sand with Ms. Anna. I had to practically push her out of this kitchen to make dinner tonight."

"Yes, ma'am. I do as I'm told. You've met my mother."

"I have met your mother, and she is wonderful. You boys always make her sound like a drill sergeant." She started bringing bowls of food out to the table as he set up plates and silverware.

"She likes you."

"Oh, that's nice. I've always seen her as a mother figure. She's never been anything but kind to me." They bumped into each other as she turned back toward the kitchen.

His voice got quiet. The space between them seemed to heat up. "I'm glad. It meant you came around a little more often, not just to see

Drew." He watched her push a hand through her hair and look up at him with those clear blue eyes.

Man, she hit all the right spots for him. His head, his stomach, his...well, he'd work on stifling that part. He lingered a moment too long when she tried to duck her head and go around him. She noticed it, he knew. *Got to stop sending signals, man.*

"And here comes the cavalry." Molly turned to catch Sam running into her arms at full clip.

"I swam in the big pool. And we played football on the lawn. And we ate icy pops from the freezer. And...can we live here, Mom?" Sam was breathless with lust for the place.

"I wish, buddy. I was thinking the same thing today. But for now, go wash up before we eat."

"Yes, ma'am." She rubbed his black curls and sent him toward the bathroom. Kerry noted she was free and easy with her movements when it came to Sam. She didn't parent with anxiety or fear. He admired her bravery, and he chided himself for his own cowardice.

"Wow! Everything looks wonderful, Molly." Hailey sat near Natalie at the table. "I totally passed out after that massage and sauna today. My muscles felt like jelly. I don't think I've ever been so relaxed in all my life. And I'm getting married tomorrow."

"It suits you." CJ leaned down and kissed her before taking the seat next to her. "Nat, you want a muffin?" CJ seemed to be settling in as a father-to-be as well.

The front door opened with the next wave of family. Hailey's parents, Sandy and Mason, along with her sister, Amy, and his own parents came through the door.

"Smells heavenly!" Amy hugged Kerry as she came in.

"I had nothing to do with it except for setting the table."

"That explains it. I thought it looked a little crooked. Probably never set a table in your life, mister."

"I've been known... No, you're right. I'm better at setting out take-out or making reservations." He pulled out a chair for his mom.

"Speaking of reservations, where are we going tonight, ladies?" Amy did a little shimmy-shake and joined the others at the table.

Hailey spoke up. "Don't tell them anything. These men will try to steal our night."

"Nope. We've got our own plans." CJ wiggled his eyebrows.

"No strippers...or lap-dance stuff...or prostitutes." Hailey couldn't even say the rules with a straight face. "I've got a spy on the inside. I'll know."

"No rules, baby. You know you can trust me. And who is this spy?"

"That defeats the purpose of a spy, now doesn't it?"

CJ looked at Kerry. He held up his hands in surrender. "Dude, it's not me!"

"We'll see what happens. But no matter what, I will be standing at the end of that beach tomorrow. No worries."

"You had better be. Otherwise, I'll be forced to have Amy hunt you down and eat you alive."

"I'll do it, too." Amy popped a green bean in her mouth and bit down purposefully before she elbowed CJ.

No one passed up anything on the table. Even the kids ate just about everything. He was going to have to hit the gym when he got home. None of it was his delight, but it was all fun to try.

Toward the end of the meal, Kerry turned to Sam and whispered, "I hear there is secret dessert."

Sam whispered back, "I know. I hope it's chocolate cake."

"I'm a pie man myself." Kerry sat back and tapped his stomach. "Does she do pies well?"

Sam shrugged. "My mom? Yeah, she does everything good."

"What are you two consorting about down there?" Molly pointed her fork in their direction.

Sam turned quickly toward Kerry, looking guilty from just the accusation. "What's contorting?"

"Not contorting. Consorting. And it ain't good, buddy. It means we've been caught." He looked down the table at Molly and smiled his best "knock her panties off" smile. "Just wondering about secret dessert."

"I told you not to ask. No candied apple pecan pie for you."

"Ugh. It is pie. Help me out here, kid."

"Awww, she's just jokin', Kerry. She'll always let you have pie."

Molly smiled at her son's charm. "It's true. He's got me there. Let's get it served up, shall we?"

Kerry and Sam high-fived. "Yes!"

Andrea and Molly served dessert while JP stood up with his beer bottle in hand. "Ok, listen up. I want to thank everyone for coming. Thank you to Sandy and Mason for sharing their beautiful daughter and granddaughter with our family tomorrow and into what is sure to be a very bright future. Thank you to Molly for this special meal, prepared in this house we've loved for so many years. And to my wife, for all of her hard work to make this wedding a success...and for loving me these many years. Sláinte."

Kerry raised his glass and smiled at Molly. She might really have baked some magic into this food – his dad was getting sentimental, over CJ no less. Well, really over Hailey, and there was nothing he could see wrong with that.

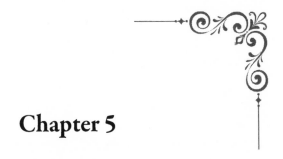

Chapter 5

TWO A.M.? Two A.M.!! Molly couldn't remember the last time she had been out at two A.M. Not since having Sam, for sure. At twenty-three, she thought that was just the saddest of statements. Something about the loss of her youth bubbled up in her mind, but she quickly swiped it away in favor of living in the moment. Too much of her story revolved around loss; it was time to change the narrative.

She and the bridal party had been to three bars, two clubs, and several shady liquor stores – for what, she wasn't sure. And they were shady even by her fairly low Chicago liquor store standards. She hadn't had more than two margaritas. She couldn't say the same for all the others.

Hailey had tried a different drink at each place and was struggling a bit for a woman who was going to look her best by tomorrow afternoon. Still, it was hard to tell if her musings were the alcohol or her heightened emotions getting the better of her. Jillian was rock solid after years of playing drums in clubs and bars. She could hold her own. Amy, on the other hand, had already had entirely too much. It was like something inside her had snapped and she was a free woman. Molly was pretty sure that "something" was courtesy of the fourth tequila shot.

They finally landed at a place called Mr. X's Shiggidy Shack on South Frigate Bay Beach. As Molly waited in the bar line for four unnecessary rum punches, Kerry walked through the breezeway and into the bar.

"Fancy meeting you here, sailor. You come here often?" He looked relaxed dressed in a linen button-down white shirt with the sleeves rolled to mid-forearm, dark jeans, leather loafers, and a large silver watch on his left wrist. *Why is that screaming sexy?*

"Only when pretty girls like you come around." He wrapped his muscular forearm around her shoulder. She tried to judge his level of inebriation.

"Where's your crew, Captain?"

"Ok, I can go with the metaphor. We had a mutiny of sorts. They're outside with the wenches." He leaned in to whisper, "Michael was the spy. He's got the Blue Banana parked outside." He slurred the word banana just slightly. "We'll make him walk the plank after he drops us off at home later."

"Scurvy-ridden bastard!" The bartender caught her attention. "Oh, four rum punches and..." She turned back to Kerry. "What does your crew need?"

"Four Caribs."

"And four Caribs. Put it on the captain's tab." She pointed a thumb at Kerry, smiled, and took the tray of drinks provided by the bartender. Kerry slapped two twenties on the bar for effect. "Let's go, man!"

The bar, or more accurately, the wood and palm-leaf shack, was filled with tourists and locals alike. They spilled off the deck and onto the beach, where two bonfires blazed into the star-filled sky. A live band played a mix of rock and reggae jams while patrons slipped out of their shoes to dance on the sand.

"Drinks are on Kerry!" Molly announced as she met back up with the now co-ed group. She spotted CJ and Hailey dancing nose to nose, lost to everything but each other.

She melted a little. "That's nice. A good way to end the night. And it's so nice to see you again, Michael." She gave him a small side hug with the tray still in her hand and then handed him a beer. "How long have you been a spy for Hailey?"

"Ah, pretty Queen Molly, there you are. Miss Hailey and I know what we have together. If she ever sees the error of her ways with that one there, I'll be waiting for her to return to my island. And me." He wiggled his eyebrows and boomed out laughter, his white teeth glowing in the otherwise darkening night.

"Michael is famous on the island for stealing your woman. Been doing it since we were kids. It's not really a fair fight. He has the island magic of Saint Kitts on his side." Kerry plucked Molly's drink out of her hand and set it down on a nearby barrel made into a makeshift table on the beach. "Let's dance before he tries to steal you away."

"Oh, am I your woman now?" *Don't answer that. Don't answer that.*

"No."

Good answer.

"Tonight, you are my wench."

Shit.

And then he was pulling her hand and walking farther out onto the sandy beach. She thought his level of inebriation was probably a seven: enough to be uninhibited, but fully aware of what he was doing.

And what he was doing was working. The man could dance. His hips moved better than she expected, but it was his hands. Oh, sweet mother of all things holy, his hands. They ran small circles over her back, slid down the sides of her skintight dress, and then pinched in with just enough pressure at her waist, always pulling her a little closer to his rock-hard body. *Damn, the way this man loves food, he must work out hard to keep those abs cut.* She'd been ashamed to admit, even to herself, that she'd been fantasizing about him since their beach excursion. He rested his forehead on the top of her head, as he was a good foot taller than her. She thought the rest of them matched up just fine.

"You look beautiful. I like this dress on you. I'd like this dress off of you."

She laughed out loud. *He might be an eight now.*

"Sorry. Alcohol makes some people angry and some people sleepy. Me? Alcohol makes me honest."

"Oh, really? Does it now?"

"Yes, I would honestly like this dress off of you."

"Well, Kerry Montgomery, you sneaky... Wait! Hold the phone."

Kerry stopped dancing and looked side to side. "What phone?"

"What time does that sexy watch say it is?"

He looked with confusion at the watch. "Two forty-five."

"Shit! No funny business."

He leaned in closer, starting to move his hips to the music again. "What'd ya have in mind?"

"No, Kerry! I was supposed to make sure there was no funny business, and now it's two forty-five on their wedding day. They can't be seeing each other right now. It's bad luck! Your mother is going to kill me!"

"Yep, you're dead." He nodded his head with more vigor than necessary. *Definitely an eight...*

"Come on!" She grabbed his hand and pulled him back toward Michael, who was sitting on the deck step talking to a pretty black woman with long braids in her hair and legs for days. "Michael. Michael! Get the banana. We're outta here!"

After ten minutes of goodnight kisses and stolen whispers between CJ and Hailey, which, under any other circumstances, Molly would have found endearing, they finally managed to send Hailey off into the Marriott. She held up Amy on the short walk to the lobby – and her guest room toilet, Molly was sure. Jillian and Drew were no help whatsoever, as they were passed out in the back row of seats. Parents of nine-month-old twins saw two forty-five A.M. often, but for different reasons. They deserved the nap. Michael drove the five of them back to the Montgomerys' house, navigating the skinny roads of his native home with ease.

Drew and Jillian disappeared up the stairs with weak waves and drowsy goodnights.

"Up to bed with you now. No couch tonight." Molly had her shoulder wedged under Kerry's armpit, pushing him up the stairs and to his bed.

"Yep. I think I'll sleep tonight. I'm gonna dream of pretty wenches and candied apple pecan pie."

"Sounds good, Captain."

IN HIS EYES, WEDDINGS were nothing but chaos. Hungover chaos amplified the hurt. He tried to stay out of it as much as possible. If he was ever getting married, and this afternoon he was seriously doubting the occurrence, he would do what Drew and Jilly had done and surprise everyone at some party or just elope. Eloping sounded perfect this afternoon.

Somehow, though, out of his mother's organized chaos and cured of their hangovers, CJ Montgomery married Hailey Wilks Powers under a brilliant blue Saint Kitts sky and all was right with the world again.

The wedding was small by Chicago society standards but fitting for the couple – CJ flouted convention at every opportunity, and one of Hailey's best qualities was her understated charm. The island itself had become a participant in the wedding, along with family and close friends from both sides. Pink, yellow, and cream flowers exploded off the tables that had been set together on the makeshift dance floor. The blue of the Caribbean Sea bordered three sides of the outdoor space and reminded him why he loved this place.

Natalie tugged on his jacket. "Mr. Kerry? Could you help me with my speech?"

He crouched down to her level. "Um, sure, sweetheart... What do you need? Do you know what you want to say?"

"I don't need you to tell me that. I got this. All I need is a boost and the mic."

Kerry chuckled as he lifted Natalie up onto the table. She patted her silver lace dress down and smoothed out the satin panel in the front. He handed her the microphone, which proved overly large for her little hand. She tapped on the mic like the performer that she was.

"Hello! Hello out there. It's my turn to talk about Mama and CJ." The crowd all exhaled a solid, "Awww," in unison.

Kerry stood next to Nat so she wouldn't step back off the table. He caught Molly's clear blue gaze and smiled. She had chosen a deep-purple sheath dress with silver heels that made her look long and lean. Her blonde hair was sprayed back off her face, making her eyes stand out larger and a darker blue than he'd noticed before.

Natalie bent forward slightly, bringing his attention back to keeping her safe on the table. "I want to tell you a secret. Shhh...don't tell anyone else 'cause secrets are for keeping. But I'm the luckiest girl in the world today. I've got two dads now. And two is my lucky number." She smiled broadly. "I know my daddy in heaven is looking down at us today. You look so pretty, Mama."

Hailey had tears in her eyes as she reached up to hold Natalie's hand, not that the girl needed any more bravery. "CJ, you might not have wanted a daughter. I don't know. You never said. Mama and me told you we were a package deal, but you never made me feel like that. I have never been a burden to you. You always make me feel like a bonus. Thank you for marrying my mama and becoming my daddy today. I love you. Deuces." She put out her two fingers, which had become their symbol for love, and held them up high in the blue sky.

Standing ovation.

Everyone settled back into their tables for dinner. Kerry helped Nat down off her makeshift stage and returned to sit next to Sunny. "She did great, didn't she?"

Sunny snapped the white cloth napkin at her setting and set it carefully in her lap. "I don't see why children should be present at a wedding."

Kerry muttered next to her, embarrassed by her lack of tact. "Well, Natalie is the daughter of the bride, Sunny."

"Yes, but what about all these others?" She waved her hand at the other side of the table, where Jillian bounced Kit on her knee and Sam held Kat in his lap.

Molly chimed in: "Kids make a wedding fun. Kind of reminds you of why you're getting married. Families, love, children..."

"In my world, darling, marriage is about consolidation of power, money, and status. Children have very little to do with it. Why are we sitting with the help again, Kerry? Shouldn't we be at the head table of your brother's wedding?"

"For the last time, Sunny, be nice. Molly is not the help, and there is no head table. You could go sit with your parents if you are bothered by the children."

"No, I'll stay with you." Sunny sighed deeply and then looked up with a renewed plastic smile. "Molly, what do you do? For a living, I mean."

"Yeah, I got that. I run a catering business, and I work in a book-store part time."

Kerry cut her off. "She's a very talented chef. She makes magical food."

Sunny's disposition perked up at the comment. "Really? Le Cordon Bleu or American trained?"

"Self-taught. Magic food can't come from muggle schools." She smirked at Kerry, who was giving her a thumbs up while trying to suppress his laughter.

"Well, did you make this magical meal we are about to eat?" A waiter set a white plate filled with the colors of the Caribbean Sea in front of Sunny as if she'd timed her question with the precision of her own Rolex watch.

"No, I'm just here as a guest. And I'm helping Jillian with the twins."

"Right. See, she is helping, Kerry."

"Just let it be, Sunny." Kerry picked up his fork to begin tasting the meal.

"I'm just interested in your new friend, love. Now, what kind of events do you cater? Anything I would have attended? Galas or art openings?"

Molly put down her fork and knife and straightened her demeanor. "Well, let's see. Did you attend Gene and Mary Anne Winston's fiftieth wedding anniversary dinner at the Moose Lodge on Harlem Street last week? If not, you missed quite an event."

The whole table laughed. Drew almost spit out his beer toward Kit.

"No, I missed that one. I was in New York last week." She turned her attention from Molly. "Kerry, that reminds me. I saw Vera while I was there. She said to give you hugs, and she was so generous to put me on her calendar for a fitting at the end of the year. I think I'll get another glass of champagne." Sunny stood, pressed down the front of her slim off-white dress, and walked stiffly to the bar.

"Kerry, what do you see in that woman?" Drew took Kat from Sam and put her in her high chair for dinner.

"She and I have a lot of common friends."

"Like Vera? Is that the Vera I'm thinking of? Did you propose to her, Kerry?" Jillian leaned in to whisper conspiratorially as she poured more water into her glass.

"Of course I didn't. Sunny sees the world through a different lens than the rest of us."

"She sure has that lens focused on you all of a sudden."

"I swear I don't know why. I haven't encouraged that. I hadn't seen her in months before this week."

"But you haven't discouraged her either. Might be the same thing to a woman like Sunny." Molly sipped her cocktail slowly. "Better make sure she knows the difference before Vera has her in white lace at the end of the year." She laughed with Jillian but then straightened. "Unless that's what you want, of course."

"Yeah. No. Ugh." Somehow, over the course of forty-eight hours and three meals, Molly had him thinking about his future more than any woman he'd ever met, including Sunny Paulson.

MOLLY FELT HIM MOVE in next to her in the bar line before she saw him. How had they gone from passing casual acquaintances, sharing Drew in common, to her recognizing his presence by the sparking energy that passed in the empty space between them?

He leaned in, wrapping a hand around her waist, and whispered, "Dance with me."

"That doesn't sound like a good idea. I wouldn't want to embarrass you in front of all your friends with my hideous inappropriateness. Is that a word?" She didn't turn her whole body to face him, just glanced back as she asked the question. Best not to give in too quickly.

"Nothing about you is hideous. And these people aren't my friends. They're my family. You're supposed to be embarrassed in front of your family. Hell, they practically live for it."

"Thanks."

"Come on. It'll help me get Sunny off my back too. You want that, right?" He pulled at her hand, and she followed...appropriately.

"Do you want that? What are we doing here, Kerry?" He placed her hand on his waist and took the other in his own as if she were a doll.

"Umm, dancing. You are quite good at it, if I recall correctly from the hazy memories I have of last night."

She chuckled and fell into a rhythm. "You're good at it too. But that's not what I meant, and you know it. You're practically engaged to another woman. You're ten years older than I am. Three days ago, I would have questioned if you knew my full name. I have nothing to offer you in any kind of relationship, if that's even what you're going for here."

"You're wrong." The live band started playing Louis Armstrong's "What a Wonderful World."

"Oh, please. Don't give me some big speech about how I have value and you're not interested in Sunny, blah, blah, blah..."

"That's not it. I was going to say I'm eleven years older than you."

"Great. But my main concern wasn't the math, Kerry."

"We're just dancing, Mol." He pushed her out, spun her in a circle, and tugged her back to his chest.

"Really?"

"Maybe. Honestly, I don't really know. But I like feeling like I feel with you."

"Well...that's a very nice thing to say. When did I become Mol?" Skies of blue and clouds of white were seeping into the cracks in her armor.

"I've been in your life a long time, Molly Anne Winters. And I don't think you've given me enough credit for what I know and what I don't know about you, your family, your history."

"Really, now? Ok, let's see, then. What is Molly short for?" He spun her in a circle again. She figured that he was stalling, but he pulled her back to his chest with the timing of the music to answer.

"Margaret, like your mom." *Bright blessed days...*

"What color dress did I wear to Drew and Jillian's wedding?" *Dark sacred nights...*

"Green sun-dressy kind of thing. See, I pay attention. Now, dance, woman." *What a Wonderful World...*

He spun her backward until she was facing the tables where they had eaten dinner. Sunny sat straight-backed, arms crossed, staring at them on the dance floor. "Your girlfriend is staring at us. She looks upset. And that's saying something through the Botox."

"Ouch! Sunny is not my girlfriend. I am going to dip you now. Try not to fall in love with me."

He makes me laugh. He makes me want. Damn, this man is trouble.

"What are you doing tomorrow morning?" He completely ignored the rest of the wedding guests dancing near them, staring at her face and tilting his head to the side when he asked the question.

"Probably packing for our flight home. Sam has school on Monday, and I've got a shift..."

He interrupted her mental list of to-dos to be completed upon their return. She chided herself, thinking, *How boring am I?* "There's somewhere I want to take you. Before we go home."

"Where?"

"I want to show you something. You and I both know you'll be up before everyone else. I'll have you back before Sam rolls out of bed."

"Hmmm, what do I need to wear for this excursion?"

"Doesn't matter. It's always warm on Saint Kitts. We'll leave at five thirty."

"A.M.? What? Really?"

"I promise. It will be worth the effort." He pulled her close, and she rested her head on his chest.

"It better be magical for that kind of effort."

"It will be. I guarantee it."

Chapter 6

"PSSST. YOU UP?" KERRY stuck his head through the open bedroom doorway and then snuck up toward the bed Molly and Sam shared. He found Molly running her hand over her son's hair and staring at his sleeping face. Sam's black curls and darker complexion, made more intense by days in the Caribbean sun, contrasted with her blonde locks and fair skin. Kerry could almost imagine that he wasn't really hers, but then he thought about how Sam favored Eric's looks and remembered the jerk who'd gotten Molly pregnant and left her without another word.

"Yes. I don't think I slept at all," she whispered back to him. "I don't want this vacation to end. Plus, I love to watch him sleep. So, I've been thinking..."

"Stop doing that. It ruins everything." He needed to take his own advice. "Trust me. Let's go."

"Where are we going exactly?" She slid out of bed, wearing nothing but underwear and a loose t-shirt.

It was no different than the swimsuit she'd worn the few days before, but Lord, did he need a minute to recover. "Throw on some shorts, and you'll find out."

He took her hand as they left the house, and he opened the car door for her. When he sat in the driver's seat, he huffed out a breath. "I just want to preface this by saying that I've never taken anyone where we're going. I have gone by myself at least once every trip I've made to the island."

"Sounds like a special place. Are you sure you want to take me?"

"Yes, for reasons I can't quite put my finger on. When we get there, I hope it's clearer."

They drove south from the house, along the bottom rim of the island, but north of the tourist beaches and scene of this weekend's debauchery. He pulled onto a small gravel road and then onto a shallow grassy area off to the side. "Up for a small walk?"

"We can't turn back now. Where are we?"

"This is Sand Bank Bay. It's not a tourist favorite, or even that special of a beach."

"Boy, good thing you're not in marketing. You're not really selling this place."

"It's never been my strength. But this beach is perfect for one thing. It is situated just right for a Saint Kitts sunrise." He felt his first twinge of excitement, perhaps the first in a long time.

He grabbed a small bag from the back seat and then took her hand again, not exactly sure why it felt right to do so. He gave it a squeeze. He was anxious to share this place with her, one he had not chosen to share with anyone else. It might be a test in his mind to see if she was the person he was beginning to believe she was or if he'd dragged her unwittingly into the spell of his favorite place.

They walked up over the sand hill and onto the still dark beach, which was deserted except for a few seagulls pecking at some washed-up seaweed. He peeked over to see her first reaction. She pushed the loose hair away from her eyes and looked out at the Atlantic. She appeared to be renewed by the breeze off the water, excited for the adventure.

"Look at all those stars. You don't get to see them from the city with all its lights. You know, when I was little, my dad would sometimes take me up into Wisconsin to go camping by a small lake up there. We'd lay under the stars and try to count them until I fell asleep. This sky looks like those nights used to." She pulled her attention away from the sky to look at him.

He broke eye contact and looked down at his feet. For a moment, he regretted bringing her to his place. He hadn't intended to make her sad.

"Thank you for bringing back that beautiful memory." His gaze shot up to meet hers in the waning darkness. "I haven't thought about those trips in so long. It's good to think about my dad when he was happy – when we were happy."

Relieved, he pulled her further onto the sand. "I'm glad you have that to remember him. I'm sorry most of the rest is tainted by what he did. You don't deserve that."

"Thank you, Kerry."

He attempted to change the mood. "We can put down the blanket anywhere. Not a bad seat in the house." He held out his arms, lifting her hand with his.

"You pick. It's your place."

"Ok, over here. There's a little sand-dune cove. It's blocked from the south wind a bit." He laid out a tartan blanket from the bag and invited her to sit. "Magic's about to start."

She didn't laugh at him, which he took as a good sign. He handed her a travel mug of coffee and sat next to her.

"You've thought of everything."

"Two sugars, one cream for you. See, I pay attention."

"I'm getting that. Why did you want to bring me here?"

"I'm not entirely sure...about anything that has happened this week, honestly. I didn't want to keep this all to myself anymore. I'm still struggling with the reasons why."

She bumped his shoulder. "This trip didn't go as I planned. Not that I was planning on you... No, that's not what I mean."

"I understand. It's been nice though – not worrying so much. Things are easy with you. Not that you're easy...that's not what I meant." He let his head fall forward, chiding himself for his lack of tact.

"I knew what you meant. You don't have to tiptoe around me. I'm not that kind of girl." She rubbed a hand along his back to reassure him. He felt the swath cool when she took her hand away.

"You mean a 'Sunny' kind of girl?"

"Well, I'm not a Sunny girl for sure. But more I meant that I've got no time for platitudes and pretty pictures of a life that isn't mine. The things that have happened to me in this life could have made me hard to be around, hard to understand. But I think I'm pretty simple. I don't have time for worrying about things I can't control. I'm more of a take-what-you-get-and-make-lemonade kind of girl."

"You are that. I bet that would be some amazing lemonade too." He smiled at her.

"We can stop thinking so much – your words – and just enjoy. We're on vacation, remember. You're supposed to vacate your life for a while, try new things – plenty of life waiting for us back home... Oh! Oh, my!"

"There she is." The sun peeked up over the horizon, just a sliver at first, then oozing out into the waves like lava, creating more colors in the already vibrant ocean.

"It's stunning." She took her eyes away from the horizon to look at him. "Magic."

"Magic." He leaned in. Their faces were inches from each other, silently asking for permission. How could they have been so close and yet worlds apart? Living in the same city for years but traveling thousands of miles to find this moment together. Sharing the same friends and family but never quite hitting the same beat until Saint Kitts.

He lifted her chin when she looked down, bridging the gap between them to take her soft lips. All of his anxieties fell away when she kissed him back. Her kiss was just like her – soft but not careful, powerful, soulful without pretense or practice. He pushed his hand behind her neck, pulling her deeper into the kiss. She ran a hand up his chest to rest on his shoulder and then pushed it up behind his neck, pulling him deeper into the magic.

"I'm sorry that this is the first time I've kissed you," he whispered between soft teases of her lips.

She smiled and laughed gently with his mouth still pressed to hers. "Only you would end such a beautiful thing with an apology. No regrets."

"End? No, ma'am. This can't be the end."

"I'm ok with that."

AM I OKAY WITH THAT? Less thinking. I'm on vacation. I'm on vacation. I'm on vacation kissing Kerry Montgomery.

He brushed both hands up over her shoulders, resting them on either side of her face, holding her gently in place. When his soft, caressing kisses stopped, she opened her eyes. He was staring at her through heavy eyes, a painful soul.

"Kerry? What is it?"

"You have changed this place for me. I can't say why, but I knew I had to share it with you."

"It's a wonderful place to be." She turned into his arms, her back to his chest, and watched the coming day rise from the water. "A wonderful place to sit and admire. Seems like the kind of spot that feeds your soul." She looked up at him. "It's perfect."

"I'm glad you came with me." He slid down next to her, resting on his elbow, making him look up at her. It was a big change of perspective as he normally towered over her with his height and strong build. A metaphor for her life, which currently felt upside down.

She leaned down to touch his lips again, unsure why she felt freer to do so from this perspective. He didn't hold back or apologize this time. She felt his heartbeat accelerate as she leaned over his chest, pressing her own to his and gaining more freedom in his body's reaction. She deepened the kiss, sliding her tongue across his and then along the underside of his upper lip. She pressed her hands over his strong chest, slipping one under his t-shirt and around to his taut back. His heated skin was smooth until she ran her nails gently along his side, causing goosebumps to travel with her fingertips. She felt him smile as he kissed her neck gently.

She gave up the idea of objecting for the sake of all things appropriate when he slowly slid her t-shirt over her head. He pushed up to sitting and pulled her onto his lap, slowly kissing her from neck to chest to breast. She felt the rising sun warm her back.

"Kerry."

He stopped kissing her to look directly into her eyes. "Molly."

"I don't... I didn't think to bring a..."

"If I tell you I have a condom in my back pocket, will you promise not to think I assumed anything here? I didn't plan this."

"I wouldn't think that. I'm as baffled by this as I think you are. I never dreamed of this kind of connection with you." She leaned down to kiss him gently. "But I'm liking it."

He reached behind her, lifting her and rolling her onto her back. Upside down again. He had a knack for changing her perspective.

He kissed down her chest to her belly while unbuttoning her shorts and sliding them off with ease.

With each kiss, she floated on the high of the sunrise, and a week in paradise, and his kindness. When he slid into her, she sailed on the breeze of the Atlantic, and new experiences, and his passion.

He hadn't lied. The place did feel like magic.

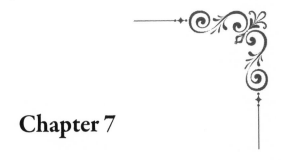

Chapter 7

DAMN, CHICAGO WAS COLD in January. Gone were the warm breezes, skimpy bikinis, and Saint Kitts sunrises. Back to reality. Still, a week after returning home, he pushed through the doors of Montgomery Shipping with a bit more gusto, even if it was brought out by equal parts frigid wind and Molly Winters. What was he going to do about her? They'd shared a special morning. That was that.

Shit.

He knew that wasn't that. Because it wasn't just the morning. If it were, he'd have left his thoughts of her on the island, just another great memory from one of his favorite places. No, it was the whole week – the conversations, the connections, the food... Damn it if he didn't want the woman for more than her cooking and sex. He wanted to share that sunrise with her. What was it about her that pulled at him? After knowing her for so long, the time spent with her had only made him want more.

Shit.

Why did she have to have a kid? He chided himself again. He liked Sam. It wasn't anything to do with him personally. He'd need to find a way to get over himself or stop things before they went any further. He'd need to do something he never did – confide in someone about his fears. For the first time in his life, he actually hoped it would change him.

His gusto now gone, he dropped into his desk chair to review the plans for the new plant they would build in the spring. It was his most ambitious project since joining his dad at Montgomery Shipping. He had spearheaded the new process, making decisions on the location, the six hundred new jobs, every piece of equipment, the entire managerial structure, and every detail down to what brand of toilet paper they'd put in the employee bathrooms. At least a thousand man-hours had been spent poring over renderings, driving the city with the commercial real estate agent to find the location, and holding more meetings than he or his staff cared to admit to make it happen. It was huge and tedious, and all he could think about this morning was Molly.

"Your two-fifteen canceled. I moved your three-thirty up to three. The architect wants a call, and you're not listening to anything I'm saying..." Janie waved a white-flag hand in front of his desk.

"Janie, do you think I could ever be a good dad?" He put his pen down and pushed the file he'd been looking at with glazed eyes to the middle of his desk.

"Well, of course you could. You'd have to get out from behind that desk more than you do. And listening is an essential skill." She tilted her head. "Where is this coming... Wait, please say that you're not thinking of having kids with Sunny Paulson. I know it's not my place, but please give yourself more credit than that. That woman does not deserve you."

"No, God no. Nothing to do with Sunny."

"Good, because she called again this morning wanting to set up lunch this week. I told her I'd get back to her assistant. Why does a woman who does nothing need an assistant? I'd like to see how that job description went. Wanted: personal assistant, must hate everyone and require no self-care whatsoever. Ugly people need not apply." She laughed at her own joke. "What prompted this anyway?"

"Nothing. Never mind. All the kids on the trip just got me thinking."

"Well, I think you would make a lovely father. Really, quite lovely."

"Thanks, Janie. Now, get me back on track. You were talking about my day..."

"Yes, the architect would like a call. The city planner meeting is on site at four thirty. I'm starting the logistics for the ribbon-cutting ceremony. We'll need press coverage and catering, and I have to find a pair of those really big scissors." This drew a chuckle out of him. She smiled at his laughter while taking notes on her yellow pad.

"I've got a name for the catering. Molly Winters runs a small catering company. I tried her food while we were all in Saint Kitts. We can't go wrong."

"Great. I've got her number. I'll set it up. You seem to have had quite a time on your vacation. It's nice to see you happy, even if it means you are a little more distracted."

"How do you read me this well, Janie?"

"Call it woman's intuition. I'm off to make some calls, and you have a ten-fifteen in Conference Room B." She picked up her notepad and turned to leave.

"Thanks, Janie. Tell Molly I said hi."

"JOLLY MOLLY, YOU BACK here again? Hope you had a good time on that vacation." Ken gave her a high five on the steps leading up to the shelter.

"Yep. Back to the grind for me, though. I've got mac n' cheese with veggies and carrot cake."

"Thanks, lady, but I don't mix vegetables with my dessert. I'm out anyway 'cause I got to find a new place to stay." Ken pushed his cart forward.

"What do you mean? What's going on?" Molly set the food down and helped him lift the cart down the last two steps.

"Big boss man and the city folks are making plans for turning our building into something else. Rumor is that they bought up this whole side of the block."

"That's terrible! What are they planning to build?"

He shrugged. "They didn't invite me to the meeting. Shocking, I know."

"I'm going in to find out what's going on. Lasagna tomorrow, Ken." She pointed a finger in his direction.

"I'm down for that. Be seein' you, Jolly Molly."

Molly took the steps two at a time despite the weight of the food she carried. Her temper was not one of her top three traits. It got her in trouble more than any of her other vices. She'd slammed out of the house, mad at her dad, the night she and Eric had made Sam. She'd spent more than one time-out in her bathroom when Sam had been a toddler, trying to reign in her own tantrums over his occasional, but still very real, bad behavior. She tried her deep breathing exercises when she reached the front door of the shelter.

Thudding into the kitchen, hell-bent on chewing out some suit with a clipboard, she set down the trays of food on the shiny silver counters. Her rage dissipated when she realized no one was there to witness her wrath. The place was empty. No suits. No city folks, as Ken had called them.

She poked her head into the manager's office. Tony was an overworked, underpaid social worker with a good heart and a reputation for being a hard-ass when needed. Tempers sometimes flew with accusations of theft or confiscation of contraband. Tony took most of it in stride. He'd given Molly the code to the door so she could bring by food whenever she had some to give. She knew he often needed it to make the budget work. Today, the office was empty. He'd be back to open the doors by five, but she couldn't stay to find out more about the situation. She needed to pick up Sam.

Returning to the kitchen, she put the food into the industrial refrigerator and went back out into the cold. Where would these men go? They had so few options in the city. How could someone just sell the land without thinking through what would happen here? She might have cried in her soup if that'd been what she'd made, but it wasn't her nature to mope.

For the second time in as many weeks, she was walking while looking down at her feet when she ran smack into the firm chest of Kerry Montgomery.

"Ouch! You look like you're ready to fight someone. What's going on?" His grin landed with a thud on top of her temper.

"Hey, what are you doing in this part of town?" Not wanting Kerry to think her anger was directed at him, she managed to put on a smile. He hadn't called since they'd returned from the wedding. She had figured a relationship wouldn't happen. Even as nice as Kerry was, she had convinced herself that there were just too many differences between them. Here he was in his business suit, cashmere coat, shiny shoes...and she was back to dropping food off at the homeless shelter in a stained white waiter's button down and needing to dash to pick up her son. They were back in the reality of living their lives in Chicago, and the differences that had faded in their tropical paradise had just smacked her in the face.

"I had a meeting. Where are you headed? How about I take you out to dinner?"

More differences – their obligations just didn't match up.

"I can't. I've got to pick up Sam. I just came by to drop off some food for the guys, and then I usually walk over to the after-school program from here."

"Can I walk with you? Or grab a cab? It's freezing out here." He reached forward and rubbed his hands over her outer shoulders to warm her up.

"It's not that far. I'll just walk it."

"How about I take you both out to dinner?" His hopefulness took the edge off her temper.

"Can't. It's a school night. He'll have some homework, and I've already started dinner."

"Here's an idea. Let's go get Sam. If, at that point, you feel like feeding me, I won't stop you."

She'd never done that before – brought a man home for a date. Was it a date? She'd always been overly protective of Sam. None of her previous dates, not that there had been that many, had ever met Sam. But Kerry already knew him, and they'd just been on vacation together. Still, she needed to make sure Sam always knew he was her first priority, and since his dad was such an asshole, she'd never let a man into his life that would hurt him in any way, physically or emotionally. She knew in her gut that Kerry wasn't that guy, but she wasn't always good with instincts. She'd made some rash choices in her life. It was too cold to fight with herself, though. "Angling for an invite, are you?"

"Maybe. I do have some pride, but I'd never turn down your food. What were you gonna make? For dinner. Just out of curiosity." He blew into his cupped hands to warm them up.

Her temper now just barely a simmer, she finally laughed at his desperation. "Lasagna."

"Argh. Really?" It came out as a groan.

"And garlic bread."

"Ooh. My kryptonite."

The last of her anger now lost to his playfulness, she agreed. "Fine. Kerry, would you like to come to my apartment for dinner?"

"Well, since you asked so nicely." He put his arm around her shoulder and pulled her into his chest. "Lead the way."

TO SAY HER APARTMENT was small would have been an insult to the word small. Minute. Microscopic. No wonder she and Sam spent so much time at Drew's townhouse. At least there, they each had a bedroom, or they had before Jillian had moved in and the twins had arrived. Here, she and Sam appeared to share a bedroom, although he did have a red racecar bed and a small screen dividing his space from hers.

Pretty sweet digs for a seven-year-old. The apartment was clean, relatively quiet until the L went by within what seemed like inches of the bedroom window, and homey. She'd managed to make a home here, and Kerry was tiptoeing a line he knew he shouldn't cross by coming into her space.

"Do you know how to play Mario?" Sam asked, interrupting Kerry's perusal of the apartment. Kerry smelled lasagna and a whiff of guilt.

"Well, I did when I was a kid. I've got to admit it's been a while."

"I got a game system, and we can play. I beat Drew a lot."

"Yeah, well, that's not saying much, kid."

Molly poked her head through the kitchen pass-through. "No video games until your homework is done, mister, even if we have a guest tonight. Go finish while I do dinner."

"Yes, Mom." He rolled his eyes at Kerry before picking up his backpack as if it weighed a thousand pounds for dramatic effect.

"I'll work on her." Kerry mussed Sam's curls as he walked back into the bedroom to do his homework.

"I heard that." She moved into the living room, wiping her hands on a kitchen towel and smelling of lemon soap. "He's being dramatic because you are here. He won't have much to finish, just some first-grade math I'm not even sure I can do. Maybe you can help. Can I take your suit coat?" His gut sank a little.

"Sure. Have you read all of these books?" The far wall of the apartment was no longer bricks and drywall. It held shelves and shelves of books, more books than the library at his parents' house. As he looked closer, the titles varied in genre from sci-fi to fantasy to parenting manuals and cookbooks. Lord, the cookbooks took up their own bookcase to the ceiling.

"Most of them. When you work in a bookstore, bringing home books is a hazard of the job. Drew builds me a shiny new bookcase when I run out of room. I guess you could say he's my enabler."

"Sounds like my brother. Do you have a favorite?"

71

"A favorite brother?" She tilted her head slightly at the question.

"No." *God, no.* "I meant a favorite book."

"That's like asking a woman to choose a favorite child...or Montgomery brother. They are all so different. I try to enjoy each for what it has to offer." *Is she flirting with me?*

"Are we still talking about books?"

"Oh, hear that? Saved by the bell. Dinner's ready. Just have to put together the garlic bread. Come on into the kitchen. We'll eat in there."

While he rolled up his dress shirt sleeves, he watched her pull the lasagna out of the 1970s avocado-green oven. She let it rest on the range while she made the bread. He took the chance to run his hands over her shoulders, giving her a gentle massage while snooping out her methods in the kitchen.

"That'll earn you some dinner."

He whispered close to her ear. "I'm sorry I didn't call this week. Life got busy as soon as we got back."

"I know. I could have picked up the phone too." She turned into his chest and looked up with forgiveness in her eyes. Forgiveness – his weakness. That was his real kryptonite. He bent forward to kiss her. His lips met hers gently, coaxing a few more seconds of quiet forgiveness. He brought his thumb up to rub along her lower lip as the kiss ended.

"Don't worry about it. It's been a busy week. Oh, you know who did call me, though? You'll never guess in a million years." She was unflappable, and he found it entirely too enchanting.

"Oprah Winfrey?"

Laughing, she turned back to finish the bread. "No, but that would be amazing. And don't stop with the hands there, mister. I can multitask. Try again."

He resumed a light rub down her neck and into the soft spaces between her shoulders. "Some famous chef who wants you to come run his five-star restaurant to critical acclaim."

"Again, amazing but wrong. Closer, though."

"I give up."

"Sunny Paulson." His hands froze.

"What? Sunny? Why?"

"I had some pretty vivid images flash through my mind too, but it turns out she wants me to cater some spring event she has every year at her parents' home."

"Really? Sunny's social? You're going to cater the social this year? That's quite the invitation."

"So, you've been? Will you go this year too?" She turned around into his arms.

"I try to find a good reason not to show up most years, but if you are doing the cooking, I'm all in. See, you must have made a good impression on her."

"Or she has absolutely no sarcasm radar whatsoever. Doesn't matter. It's a job, and a well-paying one at that. You'll have to tell me all about it." She patted his chest and moved over to the oven.

"Sure." But he didn't want to share her with that crowd, Sunny's crowd. He didn't think they deserved her. When it came right down to it, he wasn't sure he deserved to be with her, to spoil her authenticity, to ruin her grace.

"Sam, dinner's ready." She turned back to smile at him. "Let's eat. Mario waits for no man."

Chapter 8

THEY MET FOR LUNCH. She'd chosen the diner for its epic sandwiches, which she knew he would love, and for its location near the bookstore. She only had thirty minutes before her shift. But she wanted to see Kerry. She'd spent the last several sleepless nights trying to process the reasons why. Life had given her a lot of lemons. Disappointment was practically the roadmap printed on her soul. Why hadn't she learned not to get her hopes up? She didn't need him. She didn't need anyone at this point in her life. No, not need, but she sure felt the want.

"Do they make Turkish delight here?" He took her hand outside the diner and pulled her into the first booth they came to.

"Maybe for some. Maybe yours. I like their sandwiches." She picked up the overly large laminated menu and handed it to him.

"Nah, I can't see my delight being a sandwich. Unless a hot dog is a sandwich. I like a good dog at the ballpark on a summer day."

"Ah, the age-old debate. Is a hot dog a sandwich? I'm on record with a vote for no."

"Good thing we agree on that. Would have been a deal breaker for me. There's no coming back from that kind of being wrong. How about splitting a Reuben with me? I need something quick. I've got a meeting at one."

"Sure." She smiled as the waitress took their order, watching her bend down close to the table to point out the side choices on the menu to Kerry. Her cleavage practically spilled onto the table. Molly leaned in as the pretty woman walked away. "She wanted to take you home for takeout. Yowza!"

"Jealous?"

She shrugged. "I could take her."

"No brainer."

"Oh, hey. It's Ken. Hang on one second." She pushed up out of the booth and gave Ken a hug. "How are you?"

"I'm doing. Just stopped in for some eggs and bacon. These guys make the best bacon in the city."

"How is the search for a new spot going?" She squeezed his thin arm through the light jacket he was wearing, thinking both were not quite thick enough for a long Chicago winter.

"Nothin' yet, but somethin' will come up." He turned toward the booth and gave a small salute to Kerry. "I'm out."

"Ok. See you soon, Ken."

"Sure thing, Jolly Molly."

She sat back down, now opposite Kerry in the booth, and shrugged. "One of my guys."

"Competition, eh?"

She laughed out loud. "Yep. Ken was almost my date for CJ's wedding."

"I could take him."

"I bet you could. I'm worried he's not getting enough to eat. Now, what's your meeting about?"

"You know, ship stuff." The waitress set a huge plate down in between them, again leaning a little further down than was necessary. Kerry wiggled his eyebrows. "Looks good."

Molly watched Kerry take a hearty bite of the sandwich. "Wow, this is life right here. Amazing."

"They know their way around some corned beef."

"Want to go see a movie later?" He hogged the fries.

She shook her head and started to talk with her mouth full. "I can't go out. But Friday night is pizza-movie night at our house. You could come by and watch it with us. It's Sam's pick tonight. I'm gonna predict something in the Marvel Universe right now."

"Pizza? Superheroes? You? I'm in."

Wiping the Thousand Island dressing from the corner of her mouth, she smiled. "Seven?"

"I'll be there." He tossed money on the table. "I've got to go catch my meeting. How about a big smacker? Show that waitress who's boss."

"In your dreams..."

He kissed her lightly on the lips. "Definitely."

So, they could date, it seemed. She tried to wrap her brain around dating Kerry Montgomery. What would she tell Drew? Did she need to tell Drew? Maybe he already knew but hadn't said anything. It was her life, her heart. Something in her gut told her she needed to talk to him, though, and soon. Before her heart couldn't find its way out of those dreams.

JANIE POKED HER HEAD into his office just after he'd returned from his last meeting. "Line two is for you. It's Molly Winters."

"Thanks, Janie." He sat heavily in the seat. "Hey there. Why didn't you call my cell?"

"I did. It went straight to voicemail. I don't do voicemail."

"You don't do voicemail... Am I old? Is that what you've called to tell me? You don't want to see me anymore due to my being old because I still leave people voicemail messages."

"You are old, but not for that reason specifically." He liked hearing her laugh, even if it was at his own expense.

"Gee, thanks."

"We could start with the word 'gee.'" He practically heard her eyes roll through the phone. "Anyway, not really the point of my call. I'm kind of in a jam. Sam has a fever. Lillian was supposed to be working at the bookstore with me today, but she's a flake and didn't show. So, I'm alone and can't ditch. I can't have Drew get Sam, because, you know...he has twins. I wouldn't want to expose Kit Kat. And my usual babysitter is playing the slots in Vegas. Don't ask. So...is there any chance you could go get Sam? You know where the daycare is, and I wouldn't ask if there was literally anyone else I could call right now."

"Uh..."

"Kerry? Did the phone break up? Are you hearing me?"

"Yep. I heard you. I've got..." *Shit. I've got nothing.*

"It will be easy. I promise. The Tylenol is already in him." He could hear the desperation in her voice.

"Well, why can't he stay there, then?" *Can she hear the desperation in my voice?*

"It doesn't work that way. They gave him a dose, but he has to go home. You don't mess with daycare rules. You just don't. You were going to come over anyway. I'll meet you guys there at six-ish, as soon as someone can relieve me at the store."

"When you say six-ish, does that mean a little before six or a little after six?" *Desperation and fear.*

"You can totally do this. It will be a piece of cake."

"Actual cake?"

"Kerry, focus! Please go get him. I'll make it worth your trouble."

"In what way? Food or sex?"

"Wow! Ok, which one gets the job done at this moment? Because that's how my life works in these kinds of situations."

He put his head down on his desk. "Depends on the food. No, it's sex. Always sex."

She laughed again. "Just go. I told the manager that you would be there in the next fifteen minutes."

He picked up his head to look at the clock on the opposite wall. "Look who's pretty confident I'd go. What if I had said no? Or had a meeting? Or..."

"Men can be pretty simple at times. Now, go. See you at six...ish."

Well, that did not go as planned. He'd gotten distracted by her bribery. Now he was on the hook for a kid pickup. A sick kid pickup to boot. Better be damn good food and incredible sex.

He had Janie call a black car to come pick him up, which Sam thought was the best part of the whole deal. It was going to cost him, though, as the car waited outside for him to get Sam, who moved at a glacial pace due to his fever. He apparently brought every book and toy in the house with him to school on a daily basis. Most of which somehow didn't fit back into the backpack in which they'd come. And the water bottle. And his boots...my God, the winter gear alone took fifteen minutes. He thought he was finally in the clear when they sat together in the back seat for the short ride to the apartment.

"Kerry?"

"Yeah?"

"I'm gonna puke." And then he did. *Oh, the sex better be fucking amazing for this.*

When they arrived at the apartment building, he gave the driver an excruciatingly big tip before turning to Sam, who had thrown up one more time on the curb. "Let's see, kid. Can you climb the stairs to the apartment?"

"No. Can you carry me? Please?" Sam's pathetic tone mixed with the dark circles under his red eyes brought out Kerry's sympathies.

"Good thing I went to the gym this morning. Now, and this is most important, are you gonna puke on me?"

"Probably not."

"A man's word is his bond. Remember that. Hop on my back." They made it to the apartment door before Kerry realized he didn't have a key. "Is there a key hidden somewhere, buddy?"

"I have one in my backpack. First pocket."

"Ok, here it is. Why is it sticky?"

"I had a sucker in there for a while."

Kerry nodded. "Makes sense."

Lowering to his knee, he carefully let Sam dismount from his back. He watched as the boy walked into the apartment, dropped his backpack on the floor, and fell face first into his bed.

Kerry stood in the bedroom doorway. Distance was his friend. Distance and hand sanitizer.

What was he supposed to do with the kid now? He leaned into the room just enough to whisper, "Do you need anything, Sam? Are you gonna hurl again?"

"Maybe. Mom puts the green bowl by my bed just in case."

"She's pretty smart." After opening and closing each cabinet in the kitchen, he finally found the sacred green bowl and set it on the nightstand near the bed. He debated his next moves. Sweat began to bead up on his forehead. His heartbeat raced as fast as it did when he ran on the treadmill at the gym.

What would his mom do? He could call his mom. No, it was total overkill to call the pediatrician for a fever. He'd learned that in childhood, growing up with a pediatrician for a mom. All bleeding stops eventually. Life or limb, then to the ER. Neither at risk, you were lucky to get a Band-Aid. This did not qualify as an emergency. Kerry thought his anxiety might qualify. *Dude, man up.*

Ok, he'd risk it and take off Sam's boots. Done. The coat too. "Roll over, Sam. I'm gonna help you with your coat."

Sam grunted but followed commands. Before he realized it, Kerry had removed three layers and managed to strip Sam to his t-shirt and underwear before pulling the blankets up over the sleeping kid.

While he washed his hands, he couldn't help but think of how he had ended up here. From flirting with a woman he'd known practically his whole life while on vacation to cleaning up puke from a seven-year-old kid? *This is not my life.*

He opened the fridge and took out a cold beer. He figured he'd earned it. Then he put it back. He wouldn't risk drinking if he really did need to take the kid to the hospital. Not on his watch. Why was this his watch again? *This can't be my life.*

He pulled a kitchen chair into the room and sat at the side of Sam's bed. He'd just sit for a minute. Make sure of things. He looked at Sam's sweaty curls and ran a hand through his own hair. He wondered if the fear would ever go away. He suspected it wouldn't, not for him. He took some deep breaths and slumped slightly in the chair. Sam made soft sleeping noises. Kerry closed his eyes with a hand on the easy rise and fall of Sam's back. Six-ish. Seven-ish. Eight-ish.

And then she was there, waking him from his doze as she busted through the door with two grocery bags...and his heart. *This might be my life.*

"It took so long to get out of the store. I'm so sorry."

"Shhh... He's asleep."

She peeked past Kerry toward the nightstand. "Oh, he's got his green bowl. Does that mean he threw up?"

Kerry nodded slowly. "In the car. And once on the sidewalk outside."

"Ugh. I'm so sorry." She levered up on her tiptoes to kiss him quickly. "I did bring your payment. He'll be disappointed that he missed my homemade deep dish. It's his delight."

"Excuse me? You're going to make deep dish pizza? In that oven of yours?"

"Yep. Does that turn you on?"

"Oh, baby. You have no idea."

He pulled her into the living room slowly, walking backward, and eventually tugging her into his arms. The grocery bags fell to the floor as he kissed her. She reached up to hold him around the back of his neck, to dig in. He wanted to keep her all to himself, to ignore the sleeping child, to forget the fear he had of a future with her, and the growing fear he had of one without her.

He pulled away more abruptly than he intended. "When does the babysitter get back from Vegas?"

"Wow, um, weird transition. She's like sixty, Kerry."

"I don't want to sleep with her. I want to hire her. Wait, that sounded wrong too. Would she watch Sam overnight?" Laughing, she started to pick up the bags and unload them into the kitchen.

"I don't know. I've never asked her to do that. I suspect she wouldn't mind. She's back tomorrow. What did you have in mind?" She placed all the ingredients for the pizza on the counter and threw a few other things in the fridge.

"Payment for services rendered this evening. I'm expecting a pretty big tip too."

"I got that. Ok. I'll ask her about Friday. Would that work for you?"

"I'll plan it. You just make that pizza right there. I've got a feeling it will be special."

As it turned out, he and Sam shared the same Turkish delight – deep dish pizza made from a forty-year-old oven by one hot mama.

Chapter 9

HE HAD PLANNED THE date with the same attention to detail with which he did all things. But his feelings for her muddied his precision. She made him want things. She changed his perspective on things. Was that love? Was the definition of love wanting to change your life to become someone new? Or would his old fears keep him from changing anything? He tried to tell himself that if he just kept seeing her, things would fall into place. He wasn't sure what place that would be.

The date, he could control, though. He could keep his eye on the ball. He wanted to take her out somewhere special, show her his life, his home.

He wanted to show her his heart.

Squinting through the bookstore window before he went in, he saw her talking to a customer and laughing at something between them. He marveled at her maturity, her grace after years of being kicked in the shins by life. He recognized a need to protect her from further pain. She didn't need his protection, of course. He just hoped not to be the source of the discomfort.

He held the door for the happy customer to step through, and then he made his way to the counter. He had planned to pick her up directly from work to avoid any chance of getting sidelined by Sam or homeless guys or life in general. The babysitter, now returned from the clutches of Vegas, would get Sam from daycare and take him to her apartment for the night. He and Molly would have the whole evening and half of Saturday to spend together. He had plans.

"Ready to go?" He found her behind the counter, reading a romance novel with a buff guy's chest, but no actual face, prominently displayed on the cover. "Am I in that one?"

"Yep, right here." She tapped the front of the book. "The alpha billionaire with the leather and chains fetish and a harem of women looking to become his one and only."

"Sounds just like me." He kissed her quickly, leaning across the counter.

"I thought so too. Where are we going tonight?"

"Secret Chicago romance special. Did you bring your hat and gloves?"

"As instructed." She packed up her purse and picked up a small tote bag from under the desk.

"I'll take that. Our chariot awaits."

"Let me just tell Lillian that I'm going." She skipped up the stairs to the next floor of books. He paced a little. Since when was he ever nervous for a date? Maybe it was more excitement. That was a new feeling. He didn't get excited about much in his life. He took it as a good omen, but it didn't stop the pacing.

He distracted himself by picking up and putting down each book on the table of staff picks. The store had a decent selection for its size, saying something about its buyer and the staff. He wondered which ones she had recommended. He thought he'd like to try to come back and pick out a few books the next time he was in the area. Maybe they had some first editions... And then she was there, and everything else disappeared.

He reached out for her hand. They stepped out onto the street, where a long black limousine waited.

"Oh! It's lovely. Hi, Thomas. How have you been?" she said kindly to the driver, whom she'd met at other family functions.

"Very well, Miss Winters. Thank you." He opened the rear door and helped her into the elegant car. "Everything is all set, sir."

Once inside, she slapped her hands on her thighs and rubbed them back and forth. "I don't feel like I dressed appropriately for the secret Chicago romance special. I should have worn a dress."

"No, that wouldn't have worked. You look fine."

"Gee, thanks. I see the romance has begun already."

"I meant 'fine,' as in 'hot in those tight jeans.' Even Thomas checked out your ass as we got in."

"Stop. Just stop." She held up her hand. "He is too much a gentleman for that. You, on the other hand, I'm not so sure."

He reached over to take her hand and raised it to his lips. "I'm trying to be. I want to take you out for a romantic date, but all I can think about is taking you home."

"See, alpha billionaire."

"Do alpha's take their harem ice skating in Millennium Park?"

"Oh my gosh. No, they do not. I've always wanted to do that." She clapped her hands together.

"I know." He nodded, more to himself than her.

She swatted his arm. "What does that mean? How did you know?"

"You told me once. Well, you told a group of us when you were visiting over at the house. It was at Christmas one year. I was home from school, and you were pregnant with Sam."

"I remember that." She squeezed his hand.

"You said you thought skating in the park was the most romantic date you could imagine. But it would never happen now that you were pregnant."

"And I was right. It never did." She peered out the window toward the park.

"It will. I want... I want you to know that I've been paying attention. I know I've been sort of...in the periphery of your life for a while. The intensity of what I'm feeling is new, and the thoughts I'm having about you are definitely new, but...I've been paying attention. I know your story, and I want to see where this goes. I just wanted you to know that."

She turned back and caught his gaze directly. "Really? I'm...speechless. And overwhelmed."

The car stopped just outside the park. "Well, here we go. No alpha, no harem, just me."

"I'll take you." She kissed him with a quiet sigh and smiled. His heart made the leap. He might as well have handed it over right there. A happy Molly was his favorite.

They walked together to the skate rental shack. She skipped a little, pulling him forward as she walked backward, smiling and free. Her energy fed his. She was like CPR for his soul – she brought him back to life. Maybe because he didn't need to explain himself to her? No, that was lazy and filled with his own psyche. It was because she understood him already. It was easy because she made it easy to love her. Not even in just a romantic way, although he felt himself getting there too. It was easy to love her friendship, her smile, and her complete lack of guile.

"Can you skate?" she asked as she laced up her skates.

"Yeah, my brothers and I played some hockey as kids. CJ's the best at it, as much as it pains me to say. I can skate, but I stick out because I'm too damn tall for the sport. My center of gravity is too high, and it's a long way down to some very hard ice."

"I'm gonna hang on to you, then. I'm sure I can't skate at all."

"You'll be a natural. But it's not far to fall even if you're not." He laughed as he kissed her gently.

The rink was crowded with other couples on dates, kids with small walkers to help steady their skates, professionals zooming in and out, novices, and laughter. The congestion meant they couldn't skate fast, which was fine by both of them. Molly held onto his arm, leaning in for his strength. He wanted to lean back for her forgiveness. He felt like he had lured her into dating him when he knew full well that it could never be more than it was right at that moment. He needed to share his fears with her, but he found so many excuses to keep seeing her, to keep his fears quiet. He was being selfish. He hated selfish Kerry. He resolved to use their time together to make his intentions clear. And then she was there, her arm wrapped around his midsection, holding herself up as she always did, and he forgot to hate himself. She made him forget with her smile, her touch, and her joy.

On with my plan. "Want to get something to eat? I know a great place not far from here."

"No. I want you to take me home and make love to me." Ok, not the plan this early, but he could roll with it. He stopped skating and turned her into his arms. The kiss was gentle at first, like her. The heat of it quickly built in intensity, like his feelings for her. So much so that if they didn't get off the ice, he was sure it would melt below them.

He rested his forehead against hers. "Let's get out of here, then."

They made their way back to the limousine, arm in arm. Molly stopped near a homeless man petting a dog next to one of the fountains. She reached into her jeans and threw five dollars into his cup. Kerry heard him say, "Thank you, miss."

"One of your guys?"

"No, not one of mine, but I'm sure he was someone else's guy at some point. Lost his way some time back. He can use the five more than me."

"You have a good heart, Molly."

"I don't always think so. But I try to think about them in that way. I try to teach Sam that way. They all had a mom and a dad. Maybe not the best ones, but they didn't just appear out of nowhere. They have stories."

"Stories not unlike your own?" He squeezed her gloved hand, hoping hadn't stepped over a line.

"Yes, it could have been me and Sam sitting there. I'm an orphan. Sam's dad is in prison. I don't dwell on it, but I try to have some grace and be grateful. I hope you see that. I want it to be clear that I'm not dating you for your money, Kerry."

"I never would have thought that. I know you better than that."

"I feel like I'm starting to know you better. I wasn't paying enough attention before. You are kind, honest, playful even."

"I wish I hadn't waited so long, but circumstances..."

"We are right where we need to be. I firmly believe that. No regrets."

"No regrets." Although that was technically a lie. He could think of a few regrets. Before he could share those fears, they were back at the limousine. Inside, Thomas had set up two hot chocolate cups complete with whipped cream and chocolate syrup. There was a small platter of cheese, toasted almonds, and square brownies for sampling.

"How sweet! Did you do this?"

"I promised the Chicago romance tour. Thomas is going to drive down by the lakeshore for the view before we head into the city to my apartment. Unless you want a more direct route."

"No, that sounds wonderful."

SHE HAD NO IDEA WHAT to expect from his apartment, but the building fit him so perfectly that after seeing it, she couldn't picture him living anywhere else. The location was ideal, just at the crossroads of Lincoln Park and Gold Coast. The building itself was modern — all smooth surfaces, sleek lines, steel and glass. Perfect precision but not fussy. Just like him.

He peeled off layers as they entered. Coat, sweatshirt, gloves, hat — so she did the same. "Just toss it all on the table. Can I get you anything? Wine? Scotch?"

"Sure, wine would be nice." She wandered toward the quartz island and took in her surroundings, his space. The building itself might have shouted Kerry, but the furnishings inside his apartment shouted hipster roadshow. They were nowhere near his style, at least what she thought of as his style. He would be high design mixed with soft edges, functional but comfortable. Cool counters but warm touches. This was all mid-century modern, with cold white leather couches, low-profile credenzas, and even Eiffel chairs around a Tulip table in the eat-in kitchen. Not that it wasn't beautiful, but it wasn't him. She didn't think he would even fit in one of those chairs so low to the ground, given his height. She couldn't see any books on the shelves, and she knew he loved to read, especially early edition stuff. She'd started scouting some through the bookstore after they'd returned from Saint Kitts, not that she had shared that with him.

"No way you designed this place yourself. Did the interior designer know you at all?"

"Hey, now don't I look like the guy who trolls the swap meets on Saturday mornings with my gourmet coffee and man bun?" She snorted, and he replied, "I'll take that as a no."

"Really, no offense, but I bet you spent a pretty penny on this, and it doesn't even feel like you."

"Well, I was dating the designer at the time, so she should have known me pretty well. I didn't have the heart to tell her I hated it, and I haven't had the energy to change it." He handed her a glass of wine and kissed her briefly. Too briefly.

"Well, I'd have guessed warmer colors to offset the steel and glass, bookshelves up to a wood-paneled ceiling, cooler colors in the bedroom..."

"You're thinking about my bedroom? Where were you when I was getting ripped off by my designer?"

"No doubt. That kind of thing can really add up."

"Actually, I got a discount."

"I bet you did. Oh... Oh!" Her voice got low. "Is that what I think it is? Now that's beautiful." She practically knelt at the shrine that was the range in his kitchen.

"Is that a good brand? Miele, I think it's called. It has never been used."

"I'm breaking up with you."

He laughed at her joke. "So, you think my stove is sexy?"

"You are really breaking my heart here. You've had this the whole time, even after you saw my sham of an oven, and you said nothing? Do you know what I could make in this?" She sipped her wine.

"No, but I would be overly willing to find out."

She set the glass down. "After." And smiled.

"Ok. After."

She peeled off her sweater, leaving her in her best bra, the one she saved for special occasions, such as being seen by a man — especially this man – and her tight blue jeans. She watched his expression change. His striking grass-green eyes darkened – for her.

The small frame God had given her didn't leave room for much in the way of curves. The bra helped. It didn't seem to matter to him. She watched him drop down to his knees and gently kiss the center of her belly, moving ever so slowly up toward her chest. He unbuttoned her jeans and slid them to the floor before rising up to release her bra. She stood in front of him, curve-less, bared, wanting.

"I want you, Molly." It was a whisper between reverent touches and heated kisses. It wasn't frantic or lustful, but measured and sure. Never had she felt so safe with a man.

He picked her up, allowing her to wrap her legs around his waist. "I'm here because I want you too. Because I trust you."

He carried her to the bed and gently laid her back as he worked his way down her body, removing the last scrap of lace as he went. She tried to focus on his scent of teakwood and cashmere moving toward her as she watched him remove his t-shirt and jeans, revealing a taut body, maintained, she knew, with the same precision with which he pursued everything in his life.

And then he was back, covering her, working her up to a peak before pulling back.

"Kerry?"

"I'm here. I'm just exploring. I didn't get to do that the first time."

"You're good at it. Too good. I want to feel you. I need to...oh!"

"You will. Give me a chance to show you how it can be for us. You and me. I've been waiting a long time too. I want you so much."

He took his time, running his hands over every inch of her body as his kiss followed, tracing the edge of her belly, up to her breast, into the soft contours of her neck. No rush to finish. She whispered her dreams as he explored. "I never knew, but I wanted to dream."

"Move with me now. Dream with me. I always knew."

"WHAT FOOD FOLLOWS THE secret Chicago romance date? You need to up your morning-after game here, buddy." She was standing in his kitchen, wearing his oversized t-shirt and leaning into his refrigerator. As he entered, all he saw was her ass sticking out of the fridge, covered in a thin layer of cotton and as fine as any he'd seen.

"What time is it? Did I really sleep until nine? Because that would be a new record for me."

She popped back out of the fridge. "Someone wore himself out last night."

"You should have been right there with me."

"Nah, I'm younger..."

He grabbed her wrist and yanked her into his arms. "Don't say it. Just don't. I'm in no need of a reminder about how old I am or how old you're not. Do the differences between us bother you?"

"Not that much anymore. I thought about it a lot at first. You've always been so..."

"Don't say old."

She laughed again. "Responsible. I was going to say responsible. I never thought you would have looked my way. As a friend, maybe. But even that would have been unexpected."

"So, it's back to my being a snob."

"No, you've never been that. I never got that vibe at all. Sunny. Now there is a snob."

"You like to bring her up a lot. I don't compare you to her, you know. She's not my yardstick for the women I choose to bring into my life."

"No, but she is probably your future. Right?"

"I told you she's not."

She looked down at their laced fingers. "Is she...good in bed?"

"I'm really not going to have this conversation with you." It was the first time he'd seen her insecurities get the better of her.

"Ok. No more conversation, then." She crushed her mouth against his. The kiss was fierce and biting and sexy as hell. She pushed away the plates on the island and hoisted herself onto the quartz surface.

"Let's christen this kitchen. Nothing to cook in the oven, so we'll have to make due in other ways." He worked the t-shirt up to take her breasts, to feast on her body. He couldn't let her go even if it was wrong to hold on. She pulled him in. She gave herself to his desire, and he wouldn't have been able to stop even if the place had suddenly lit up in flames.

He'd never look at the kitchen the same way again. He'd never look at it without thinking of her.

Chapter 10

"I'M JUST SAYING, IT'S not a good idea. You guys don't want the same things." Drew pulled a jar of sweet potatoes out of the cabinet.

Molly folded towels at Drew's kitchen table while he plopped Katie into her high chair. She handed him a new, dry bib.

"Damn, these kids can drool."

"Don't swear in front of your children." She slapped the towel she was folding for effect.

"They're eleven months old. I think it'll be ok." He popped the jar lid for effect.

"Yeah, but you'll blink, and they'll be sixteen, to use your words against you."

"Katie would never talk that way to me. Would you, my little Katie girl?" He made babbling noises toward his daughter.

"Every dad wears blinders. Anyway, what's wrong with Kerry and me seeing each other? What's so different about us?" She felt so connected to him after last week's...whatever they were calling it.

"This is already happening, isn't it? You guys already hooked up." He pushed the spoon through the orange mush and fed his daughter. "Jeez, Kerry knows better."

"That was better. You caught yourself that time. I don't need you to be my protector, Drew. I'm not frail and wilting. I know my own mind."

"Kerry might be out of his." Little Chris squealed from his bouncer seat. "See, he agrees. Listen, all jokes aside, maybe things have changed for him, but..."

"But, what? Spit it out, man." She had walked over to the drawers and was putting away kitchen towels, as familiar with Drew's kitchen as her own.

Drew huffed out a breath. He set down the spoon and looked at her squarely. "I have a feeling I'm going to regret this, but...Kerry doesn't want kids. Never has. He's made it pretty clear that he won't have kids. Not that he doesn't like them. Just that he...wouldn't want them." He reached up and squeezed her arm – an attempt to console her, she knew.

Chris threw a rattle on the floor with a bang. She turned away and walked back toward the happy boy bouncing in his saucer near the table. She was not going to let her emotions get the better of her. "But he likes Sam. And we're not in anywhere near that kind of relationship."

"I said he likes kids. I'm sure he likes Sam very much. We all love Sam. But I can't see him wanting to move forward in a relationship where a kid was involved. I'm not saying this to hurt you. I'm trying to save you some hurt. He was pretty f–"

"Uh, uh, uh." She interrupted his potential swear with a wagging finger.

"He was pretty *screwed* up after Bettina died. He has never really recovered, I don't think. Can't forgive himself. He could build a ship from stem to stern, let it set sail with a full crew, negotiate with pirates for Chri... goodness sake, but he will never let himself be responsible for a kid again. They're his trigger."

"He's never said anything about it, one way or the other. But he's obviously not said anything to you about us either. Is he hiding it? Me?" She leaned against the kitchen island and crossed her arms.

"It's not like Kerry to hide something like this. I can say it must be either important or painful to him if he doesn't want to share it with anyone. That's always been his deal."

"He's important to me too. But never more than Sam. Maybe he's changed his mind about kids?"

"Maybe. I just don't want to see you or Sam get hurt." He picked up Chris and tucked him onto his hip.

"I'd never let that happen."

"I know, mama bear." Drew pulled her to his other hip in a hug and kissed the top of her head. "I know."

"HEY, KEN. HI, TONY. How are you guys?" She had a lightness to her step, carrying in leftover chicken parmesan, garlic breadsticks, and garden salad from a successful bridal shower she had catered the day before. She was new enough to this business to make more food than was technically required, just in case, but she'd been a woman long enough to know that women rarely ate much at bridal showers. She had tons of leftovers.

Tony appeared happy to see her. "Hey, Molly. Thanks for this. We can certainly use some positivity around here today."

"Why? What's up?" Ken seemed sullen. She worried that he hadn't found anywhere to stay.

"You really dating the suit?" Ken crossed his arms and sat in a dining room chair in a way that reminded her of Sam having a tantrum.

"Who? Kerry? Yeah, something's going on there." She looked back and forth between the men. "Why? You jealous all of the sudden?"

Ken lowered his voice. "You never seemed like a traitor to me."

She set the food containers down on the counter. "Excuse me? How am I a traitor? I just brought you dinner, like I have almost every day for the last two years."

"Sleeping with the enemy." He shook his head and turned in his seat.

"I'm so confused." She looked from Ken to Tony for clarification.

"Leave it, Ken," said Tony. "It's business and none of yours."

"Would someone please tell me what he is talking about?"

"He really shouldn't be talking about anything." Tony sighed. "He says you're dating Kerry Montgomery."

"Yeah, so?"

"Mr. Montgomery's company...they're the ones moving us out, taking over this space. He's mad that you didn't tell him."

"Well, shit. I didn't know." There wasn't enough room in the building for the amount of steam that suddenly built up in her body. She started pacing. "That bastard. Not you, Ken. I'm talking about Kerry." He hadn't said anything. He knew, and he hadn't told her.

Tony tried to talk her down in his calmest social-worker tone of voice, using his de-escalation toolbox. "We'll find some space. I don't know where yet. The city folks are working on it."

"Yeah, I'm sure that'll be the highest priority for everyone involved. Meanwhile, where will our guys go, Tony?"

"Molly, I love that you are so invested in these men and their outcomes. Really. I am too. But we've got to work within the system we have. Unless you've got a few extra million hidden somewhere. I know I don't. We'll be ok, but we have to work the problem from the inside."

"Nothing about this is ok. I'm going to talk to him."

"Please don't do it while you are this worked up. That won't help anyone, especially not in a new relationship."

"Tony, I wish I had your grace. I thought I knew him. I thought he was being honest. I thought he was safe." She sat next to Ken and rested her head against his shoulder. "I'm not a traitor for falling in love. A fool maybe. But I sure as hell won't be lied to. I won't let them do this to you, guys. I won't let him get away with this."

"You sure you're talking about us now?"

"I'm not sure of anything anymore."

SHE BURST THROUGH THE door, past Janie talking on the phone, and blew into his office like a tornado picking up speed and low-lying debris. "You're the suit? You're the bastard who's pushing my guys out to build a shopping mall or a Burger King or one more of whatever it is we don't need in this city?"

"Whoa! Molly, slow down. I'm not building anything of the sort. It's a business deal. And as you can see, I'm in a meeting here."

The man at the table appeared to be in his early fifties, with salt-and-pepper hair pulled back into a ponytail and wearing an ill-fitting brown suit that looked like it had last made an appearance in the late 1970s. She acknowledged him with a head nod. "Hello there."

"Hi, mate."

She turned back to Kerry. Her temper couldn't be curtailed by pleasantries and manners. "Does he know what a jackass you are? What you and your company are planning to do to the homeless population of this city?"

"Excuse me?" He turned toward her and tried to lower his voice. It came out as a growl. "You need to calm down. You don't know what you're talking about. Go outside, and I'll talk to you when I'm done with this meeting."

She stomped her foot like a child in a grocery store denied the candy in the checkout lane. She'd been there more than once – she knew the stance. "I'll wait here."

The business associate stood. He spoke with an Australian accent. "I can see you have something to sort out here, mate. We are basically done anyway. I'll email you the changes you've requested, Mr. Montgomery. No worries." He quickly rolled up the blueprints on the table and turned to her with a coy smile. "Nice to meet you, miss." Then he shimmied out of the office and out of her path.

"I am so sorry, Mr. Allister. Thank you for coming today..." He turned to Molly with a storm brewing in the green of his eyes. "Well, that was embarrassing. To answer your question, if there was one amongst the epic childish tantrum you just performed, Montgomery Shipping is building a new state-of-the-art plant, which includes six hundred new jobs and a larger port for all the goods you want to buy in those shopping malls and Burger Kings you mentioned so gracefully when you came in." He started picking up papers from the table and shoving them into folders, seemingly at random.

"And what about my guys? That shelter is their only home."

"Your guys? They're not your guys, Molly. They will be relocated. No big deal." He turned away to stack some of the papers still left on the meeting table.

"Not to you."

She watched him from behind. He huffed out a breath, trying to rein in his own temper. "It is a very big deal to me. I've worked my ass off on this deal."

"I'm sure you have. It's what you do. Clean, precise, just cut people out, get what you want, and move on."

He spun back to look at her. "Wait one minute. When have I ever done that? Is this really about the shelter? I've never seen you this angry."

"Of course it is. No...no, it's more than that." She started circling the meeting table, picking up more steam as she went. "You don't want us. I'm an us. I'll never be just me again as long as Sam's on this earth. And you don't want an us. You don't want a kid. Well, guess what, buddy? You don't get me without him. He's pretty great, you know."

He walked over to close his office door, and all the fight left him as he did. His voice returned to a normal volume, though it was clogged with anger. "Please sit down. You're making a scene. I don't want to have this conversation here."

She continued to yell. "You don't want to have this conversation at all! It's been weeks, Kerry. Weeks! What did you think would happen? I'd somehow miraculously not have a kid anymore? I'd fall in love with you and give him away?"

His eye shot to hers. "You're in love with me?"

"I was. As much as I could be with someone hiding something like this from me."

"Shit. I knew I let this get too far." He sat and ran his hands through his hair as if making a decision. When he spoke again, he sounded quieter, more thoughtful. "I can't do it. I tried, but I can't. I never wanted to hurt you or Sam. I've spent years pushing you away to not have this conversation right here. I'm not a father. I don't want to be a father. I'm not going to do that to another kid."

"She wasn't your kid. From what I can see, everyone has forgiven you, assuming there was even anything to forgive. It was an accident. Why can't you forgive yourself?"

"Don't pretend to know what this feels like. You don't know. No one knows."

"Ok, then wallow in it as long as you want, but don't pull me into it. Tell me this. Why did you start this? It's not like I threw myself at you. You pursued me."

"Yes, I did."

"And Sam's been here the whole time."

"Yes, he has."

She threw her arms in the air and circled the chair she didn't want to sit in. "How many chances did you have to stop seeing us? To tell us you didn't want in?"

"Too many. Every day, I know. I'm sorry."

"That's it? You're sorry?" Her voice broke, stuck in her throat for just a moment. Then it reemerged, quieter but resolute. "Don't call me, Kerry. Don't contact me through Drew or your family or any of the million ways we are connected. I see the differences in us so clearly now. I see you clearly now."

Chapter 11

"DOES IT MAKE US OLD that girls' night out is now moms' night in?" Jillian set the large popcorn bowl down in the middle of her and Drew's polished wood coffee table before falling into the last cushion on the sofa. She was already in pajama pants and a short t-shirt. "Worse, I don't even care that the guys are out for St. Patrick's Day and we somehow got suckered into watching the kids. I'm tired."

Molly snorted. "Well, if staying in and watching kids makes us old, then I've been old since age sixteen. I've never been to girls' night out. Every day is moms' night in for me. Well, except for Hailey's bachelorette party."

Hailey dropped off the stairs into the living room. She'd tucked Natalie in next to Sam and checked on the twins while Jillian had made the popcorn. "That's unlike you. You're usually the most positive person I know. What's going on?" Hailey sat in the armchair opposite Molly.

She looked down at the paper napkin she'd inadvertently shredded. "I broke things off with Kerry."

Both women sat straight up and looked from Molly to each other.

"You had *things* with Kerry?" Jillian almost let the popcorn fall out of her mouth. "You've been holding out on us? Give it up, sister!"

Molly shrugged like it was old news. "It started in Saint Kitts."

"Wait, what? Saint Kitts? At my wedding? And you are just now sharing this fact?" The two women laughed in unison.

"It wasn't like I was hiding anything. Not really. Shoot, maybe I was. It was so...nice."

Jillian sat back with her wine and took a small sip. "Casual sex usually is. Or it used to be, as far as I remember."

"Girl, kids will tear you up and spit you out."

"Said the newlywed." Jillian pointed at Hailey. "Your sympathies are weak, sister-in-law. You two are still rabbits, and I know it."

Hailey smirked. "This is about Molly. Now, tell us. How did this happen?"

"It was vacation. You guys kept telling me I was on vacation."

"I don't think this is our fault."

"No, I'm not saying that. We just...connected."

"Sounds hot." Jillian wiggled her eyebrows.

"Not like that. Well, some like that, but we got to know each other, and it was good. Until it wasn't."

Jillian grabbed a handful of popcorn and spoke through a mouthful. "Wait. First the good stuff and then the he-did-a-stupid-man-thing stuff."

"Why did it take so long for him to figure out what a catch you are? He's known you practically all his life." Hailey poured herself a glass of wine and settled in for the details.

"I never really thought about him in that way either. There are so many differences between us. He's more than a decade older than me."

Jillian shrugged. "Makes no difference if the other stuff is right."

"And he's got money, not that I'm struggling, but I'm no Sunny Paulson when it comes to cash."

Hailey pointed at Molly. "Thank God for that. What a... Never mind. This isn't about her. This is about you."

"Most of the time, I feel like I'm just making it day to day, still finding myself along the way. He's got life all figured out. Right?" Molly looked to these two women who were more than her friends. They were her sisters.

"From the outside, it can look like he's got it all sorted out. But I always get a lonely vibe from Kerry. He wants more than he lets on –

more family, more play, more life. I always think he doesn't give himself those things for some reason."

Hailey sighed. "It's Bettina. I swear she haunts him. He can't forgive himself for her death, so he doesn't let himself really live."

"But it was so long ago. You think it still gets to him?" Jillian pushed the popcorn bowl toward Molly.

"Oh, it's definitely still there. He's pretty screwed up when it comes to kids. He said he's been waiting for the right time to tell me he was interested. Well, buddy, you lost your chance now." She swigged down the rest of her wine and poured a second glass.

"No! Don't skip the good stuff. I'm living vicariously here. Was he good? I'd imagine he's pretty good. Not that I imagine sex with Kerry. But come on. Give a girl something."

Molly laughed for maybe the first time in two weeks. "He's...thorough. Top to bottom, ladies." She nodded slowly.

Both women groaned. "Thorough is gooood."

"I haven't had thorough since before the twins. Now it's all, 'Quick, Drew, get it done before one of them wakes up.' Thorough sounds exquisite."

Molly threw the shreds of her napkin down on the coffee table. "If you're done coveting your brother-in-law, I can tell you it's over. I would never have expected him to lie, but he did...daily."

"Lied about what?" Hailey turned serious, seeing how emotional Molly had become.

"He never wants kids. Can't see a life as a father. But he led me on. Every day that we were together. He had a million opportunities to tell me it wasn't anything he wanted, that Sam wasn't part of the plan. I'd have picked up my heart and moved on."

"I'm sorry, Molly." Jillian rubbed her hand over her sister's back.

"I never see Sam as a mistake. He's been a gift to me, but I've never been so confronted by my own insecurities. It's like he used me for sex, because, obviously, I'm ok with that since I have a kid, and then he can just move on without a second thought. Like he was never invested from the start."

"I'm not defending him, but that doesn't sound like Kerry to me. He's an honest guy. Maybe he really didn't intend to let things go so far. He got caught up in the moment, like you said."

"I knew I shouldn't trust anyone."

"And that doesn't sound like you, Mol. You are self-sufficient, yes. But trusting him with your heart is different than relying on him or needing him. Did you fall in love with him?"

She sighed. "Top to bottom."

THE HARSH KNOCK ON his apartment door at nine P.M. jarred Kerry out of the light sleep he'd fallen into lounging on his couch with a copy of *The Martian* resting open on his chest. "Kerry! Get your ass out here!"

Already in a white t-shirt and cotton pajama pants, he had zero interest in Montgomery Men's night out, even if it was St. Patrick's Day. He opened the door to Drew who had apparently started the festivities without him, not that he cared. "Jesus! What?"

"Men's night. Get dressed. Where do you hide the Jameson?" Drew walked past him, into his apartment, and started opening cabinets.

"Looks like you've already been into it. Where's CJ?"

"Paying the cab. Why aren't you ready to go?"

He left the door slightly open and followed Drew into his living room. "Because I'm not going."

"Like shit, you're not. It's your day man. We're going to the Kerry-man. It's your bar. You always want to go out on St. Patrick's Day."

"I don't feel like it this year. You guys go with my blessing. Have fun."

CJ pushed through the door. "Why the hell aren't you dressed?"

"Because I'm not going anywhere. What's with you two?"

"Brother, you are going to the Kerryman on St. Patrick's Day and you are going to get drunk like the fake-Irish bastard that you are. Why did mom and dad name you Kerry anyway?"

"I don't know. Go ask dad."

CJ put his arm around him and hugged him in tight. "Brother, Brother..." Shit, it was sappy CJ. Clearly, their festivities had started hours earlier. He was beginning to think he might need to go along, not for the liquor or the ill-advised female companionship but just to make sure they got home at the end of the night.

Drew pointed with an unsteady finger. "Get dressed. We're going to the Kerryman and you're going to get drunk, Kerry Montgomery. You're going to get drunk and meet a woman and bring her home to this impeccable apartment and have impeccable sex." He was already slurring his c's so it sounded like a chicken "pecking" each time he said it.

"How long have you two been in the sauce today?" He started to find them amusing. "And where are your wives?"

"They are watching our kids. We have kids, Kerry." Drew tapped on his chest as he said it. "And I thought you were the old fuddy-duddy."

"Thanks. So somehow you've managed to get your wives to stay in on St. Patrick's Day and we're to go out and get stinking drunk and hook up with women?" He shook his head knowing full well that was not the plan.

CJ started paying attention. "No, not us. Just you. I'm not allowed to do that anymore. I don't think anyway."

"No, you definitely are not allowed to do that anymore. Ok, I'll get dressed and we'll go if only because it's Men's night and you two need a babysitter already."

"Good. Let's go." Drew finally found the liquor cabinet and pulled out the Jameson.

"Hold your horses, asshole. It'll take me a minute."

"Ok. You go get pretty, and we'll have some of this." He held up the bottle and walked to the kitchen for glasses.

Shit. His night was about to be consumed by babysitting his little brothers, something he'd done his whole life – and honestly, that he thought would be over when each married the girl of their dreams. Bastards. Here he was, putting on a good shirt and slacks that would probably end up puked on before the night was over, if not by them, then by some other idiot drinking too much green beer. He thought of Sam, of when he had been sick, and that made him think of deep dish pizza and Molly. Maybe he would get drunk and hook up with someone. He didn't have to be the responsible one all the time.

What was she doing tonight? Whatever it was, he thought he wanted to be there with her, not here with them. He heard a crash from the living room. Shit.

The Kerryman was packed; even the outside patio was full, as the weather had broken just days earlier and fifty degrees in Chicago is considered almost perfect drinking weather, especially after a long, cold winter. The place was as close to an authentic Irish pub as they had in the city. The owner, a real Irishman named Pat O'Callahan, had been one of Drew's first clients, with a beauty of a boat he'd named *An Irish Wake*. Kerry knew he'd imported his chef directly from the island itself, and although food wasn't on the agenda tonight, he thought that he would have liked to have brought Molly here for a meal.

The shiny mahogany bar called like a siren to him. After a quick handshake with Pat and with three Guinnesses in hand, he found his brothers at an outside table with several young, drunk women wearing knee-high socks, short skirts, and green half-shirts that said stupid things like "Irish You Were Naked" or "Let's Get Ready to Stumble." It was gonna be a long night.

"Hey! Ladies, this is our brother. He's single and lonely."

"Hi, single and lonely, my name is Patty."

"I bet it is. You can lay off Patty. I'm neither of those things. Move on." He motioned with his elbow as his hands were full with beer.

"Come on, girls. These old guys are boring." They raised their middle fingers as they walked away.

CJ chuckled and clapped him on the shoulder. "Well, look there. Our table just opened up. You didn't have to be rude though, Kerry. Since when aren't you single and lonely? You seeing somebody?"

Drew pulled up a stool and drank from his Guinness. "He's dating Molly, or was dating, from what I hear."

"How did you know?"

"It wasn't a military secret, Kerry. She told me."

"You talked to Molly? When was this?" He felt his voice getting higher, but he didn't care.

"I don't know. I talk to Molly all the time. She was my friend before you two started up. Don't get your panties in a twist. Probably two weeks ago."

"Wait. You were hitting on little Molly?" CJ looked at him as if he'd grown a second head.

"He wasn't just hitting on her." Drew motioned toward Kerry with his full drink, causing it to dribble down the side of the glass.

"Shut up, Drew. I don't need you blasting my business to the world."

"She came to me, man. I just told her the truth."

"What truth is that exactly?" He already knew the answer, but he wanted to hear Drew admit it.

"That you don't want kids. I didn't want you to break her heart. She's had enough bad shit in her life."

"So, you get to decide who she sees? I can't believe it was you. You fucking bastard!" Kerry pushed off his stool and landed a right cross before Drew could even put down his drink.

"What the fuck, Kerry?" Drew wiped at his chin while blood oozed from the corner of his mouth. Then he lunged for Kerry, grabbing him by his shirt and landing his own punch to his ribs.

"Hey, hey! You two are gonna get us kicked out of here. Pat's looking at us."

"I take it she dropped your ass. Serves you right for being so high and mighty. She's too good for you."

They struggled together before Kerry pushed off. "You're right on that one. I'm out of here. Get your own asses home."

"Kerry! Don't go," CJ pleaded.

As Kerry walked away, he heard Drew say, "Let him go. We don't need him."

"Yes, we do. I was living vicariously through him tonight. Now I'm stuck with your married butt."

"Thanks." Drew held his cold glass to his split lip. "Bastard can punch."

Kerry woke up the next morning with a sore hand and bruised ribs. The pain was a good reminder of the chink he'd allowed in his armor. No more moping. It was time to move on with life, even if he might regret it – and he was probably going to regret all of it. He reached for his phone.

He typed the invitation slowly: *How about dinner tonight?*

Her answer was quick: *Been waiting for you to come to your senses, love. She wasn't good enough for you. The club at seven.*

Chapter 12

SUNNY'S SOCIAL REPRESENTED everything Kerry hated about Chicago society and his reluctant place in it. But he knew Molly would be there, and he didn't hate that. They had not seen each other since she'd slammed into his office three months earlier, thrown him to the ground, and driven over his conscience with her bulldozer — twice.

That wasn't entirely true. He saw her every time he walked into his kitchen.

He wandered the grounds in front of Sunny's parents' home, dutifully inspecting the tables and chairs, as Sunny had instructed. She was busy making sure every flower in every arrangement was without fault. He thought the florist might stab her with one of those flower picks before the end of the day. Honestly, an urgent trip to the emergency room would be preferred over spending what was sure to be many tedious hours air-kissing cheeks and making small talk with people he didn't care to know.

Their relationship in the last weeks had revolved around the social. He and Sunny had spoken of precious little else, but to be honest, he'd heard only about ten percent of it. He had somehow successfully navigated the relationship without engaging in the drama, which was saying something because Sunny was all about the drama. He thought it probably said something about his commitment to her, or lack thereof, but Sunny either didn't care or didn't want to rock the boat. She was getting what she needed – an appropriate suitor and his parents' money if she stuck it out long enough. It turned his stomach at times. Was this really his life? His path? He felt like a rowboat bobbing in the harbor. He'd lost sight of his lighthouse and was moving in circles, searching for home.

When he finally crossed paths with Molly at the social, she wasn't dressed in a chef's apron or her usual white waiter's button-down. She wore a simple navy and white polka-dot dress with white high heels and silver earrings shimmering on each side of her pretty face. Her hair had grown out a bit. She'd twisted it up today, for practicalities, he was sure, but the style elongated her neck and made him want to leave a trail of kisses along its length. He had no right to want.

He stopped to watch for a moment as she was directing the catering staff and carrying a small clipboard. Sam sat on a folding chair in the back of the outdoor kitchen, playing a video game in a freshly ironed shirt and slacks.

"What's on the menu?" Kerry said in a light tone behind her, but he noticed that she froze at the sound of his voice.

"Heavy hors d'oeuvres and Champagne punch," she said as she turned to face him.

"Hey."

She looked down at her clipboard. "I don't have time for 'Hey.' Things are moving fast here in the kitchen. Please go out with the other guests."

He felt no forgiveness in her today. Her eyes were filled with hurt, with judgment, with anger. She was entirely right, of course.

He gave a short wave toward Sam, who'd looked up from his game and smiled in his direction. "You brought Sam with you?"

"Yes, I cleared it with Sunny. I didn't have anywhere else to send him today, and she was fine with it. A little too fine, actually. She's the one who encouraged me to bring him."

He knew Sunny was well aware of the status of their relationship and the reasons they were no longer together. He shouldn't have told her, but then again, he shouldn't have gotten involved with Sunny again after his bulldozing. She'd pounced faster than a cat on a laser pointer. He knew she'd encouraged Molly to bring Sam to rub salt in his wounds. To remind him of the reasons he and Molly could not have a future.

"He's a good kid."

"Yes, he is. The thing is, Kerry, I need to do my job here now. I don't have the time, or the inclination, honestly, to talk to you about Sam or us or anything else."

Sunny sauntered into the kitchen setup tent. She wore a Chanel suit and one of those fascinator hats like she was royalty. "Kerry, so happy you made it, love." No air-kisses for him today. She kissed him on the lips in a stunning display of cattiness. "Molly, it looks great. Let's just hope it tastes good. If so, we might have you help with a future event." She swung an arm through Kerry's. "Have you done any weddings yet?"

He watched Molly inhale quickly and then recover just as fast. "No, but I love weddings." She punched him in the arm, one of those chucks you give when you're happy about something, except it was fierce and hurt more than he might have expected from such a small person. "You two kids let me know. Let's get today done, and we'll talk, Sunny."

"Make sure you keep an eye on your boy there. Don't want him eating all the food or mingling with my guests, now."

"Sunny!" Kerry was mortified by her snobbery.

"It's fine, Kerry," said Molly. "He'll stick to the kitchen. He won't be any trouble." She turned at the call of her name. "Coming, Fran. I've got to go. Enjoy today." She whisked off to help one of her waitresses for the day with a tray of quiches, leaving him with a trail of fresh citrus scent and his memories.

Spring in Chicago could be hit or miss, weather-wise. If Sunny could have purchased sunshine directly, he wouldn't have put it past her. She'd obsessed over the weather reports for the past forty-eight hours. Luckily for him, it was an exceptionally warm, bright day, and he wouldn't have to hear any more about it.

His parents were attending, as were Sunny's, along with about half of the Chicago society crowd that mattered to her. She'd had several fits over the last few weeks when the turnout looked like it might be down this year. Her ego had recovered as she'd convinced herself that the quality of the attendees had improved from last year, even if the quantity had not. He wondered how you measured the quality of a guest, but he quickly realized that the size of their bank account was fully measurable and probably her yardstick for such an analysis.

He was thrilled to see his mom as the afternoon entered full swing. Safe conversation, honesty, substance. He was a man drowning in sand in a desert of superficiality. Andrea Montgomery glowed in a light-green sundress and matching hat. She pushed her arm through his and walked along the deck as they talked. "Nice day. Handsome son. I've got it pretty good today."

"Hi, Mom. You look nice too."

"I was just thinking that this menu is special. Don't you think? I particularly like these small mushroom caps. I'll have to stop and compliment the chef at some point."

"She's there." He stopped walking and pointed toward the edge of the lawn where Molly was supervising the wait staff.

"Of course. She looks very pretty today. Don't you think? Have you spoken with her?"

He turned back toward his mom, removing Molly from his line of sight. "Briefly. She doesn't want to talk to me. I don't blame her."

"Does she know what you've done?"

"I don't know. I doubt it. If Sunny comes looking for me, tell her I'm inside or making a food run, or hell...I don't care what you tell her. I'm going to wander by the lake a bit. Clear my head." When she started to object, and he knew she wanted to talk more about Molly, he simply leaned in and kissed her cheek. "Leave it, Mom. She deserves better."

"I don't want to hear anything of the sort. You are a good son and a kind man. Mistakes don't define you, Kerry. She knows that better than most people. Did I see Sam here earlier?"

He turned to look toward the kitchen tent. "He's hanging out with her today. Maybe I'll stop over and see if he needs anything."

"Good, do that. I see your father talking to Arty Paulson. I have to go save him."

"I thought you liked Sunny's dad?"

"I don't dislike him, but he gloats about his golf game, which gets your father worked up. Nobody needs that today. He's a decent man, but he's not our people. Neither is his daughter, if you have any thoughts in that direction. You know that in your heart, right?"

"My heart and my head don't seem to match these days."

"Go walk by the lake, then. Always works for me. I'll catch up with you later."

He moved through the crowd toward the outdoor kitchen and entered the tent toward the back, where Sam had been sitting earlier. The boy's video game lay on the chair, but he was nowhere to be found. Probably had gone in search of food. Kerry couldn't blame him.

As he walked down toward the lake, spring sunshine sparkled off its waves. The lake...she was a fickle mistress. She was both mother and maker in his eyes. She gave and she took.

Despite the day's warmth, he knew the water would still be frigid. He remembered the way his feet had gone numb when he'd searched those same waters for Bettina on the day of the accident. He never looked at the lake without thinking of her. As much as he could, he tried to remember her smile and her spunk. Most of the time, he just thought of the panic. He remembered how he'd tried to recall the CPR sequence while he'd scanned the churning waters, just in case he could get to her. He remembered the fear he'd felt buzzing through his fingers when he couldn't see her, when he never found her body.

He almost turned back, unable to clear his head with the swirling memories of the lake so close, but something just caught his eye. When he looked again, he could see it was an orange kayak tipped upside down, floating offshore about thirty yards. At first, he thought it must have blown loose from the boat dock.

Then he saw him.

A child, a boy from the look of the clothes he wore, was thrashing next to the small vessel, reaching up to grasp the side to pull himself up from the water. But there was no grip. He was failing.

Instinct overtook panic. He tore off his suit coat and slid out of his shoes. Diving in, he felt what must have been ice crystals tearing across his skin, and he began to swim toward the color orange. *What's the sequence? Is it two breaths and ten compressions? No, he's a kid. Kids are different. Keep thinking. Keep moving.*

He swam the circumference of the kayak. *Where did he go? He was right here.*

Diving under, he came up into the air trapped beneath the boat. He turned in a circle, paddling to keep himself afloat in the icy waters, churning his legs to stay above the panic.

Huge breath and back under. The water remained clear this close to the shore, but it was still deep. Panic made him feel blind. Then a reflection – silver metal reflected up into his line of sight. He dove down to the lake floor. It was a belt buckle. His legs felt like anchors as he pushed off the rocky bottom. But then he was pulling the boy up, up and out of the water, dragging the boy toward the shore. Everything was numb – his feet, his fingers, his mind.

Kerry hauled him to the rocky shoreline, turned him onto his back, and saw his failings looking back at him. Sam. It was Sam, and he wasn't breathing.

He screamed for help. "Call 9-1-1! Get help!"

"Now," he whispered to himself through raspy tears.

Breath. Breath. Pulse.

Breath. Breath. Pulse.
Start compressions.
Breath. Breath. Pulse.
Breath. Breath. Pulse.

"Please. Please, Sam. I love you, Sam." His arms started to get weaker. The cold of the water was settling into his muscles. His movements became stiffer, more ragged. He wasn't sure how much longer he could go on. Would help ever come? When would they save him?

When would they save Sam?

And then his mom was at his side, yelling his name and pushing him toward the grass. "Kerry! Sit back. I'll take over."

"Take over. Yes, take over." He struggled up and away. Someone wrapped a blanket around his shoulders. He sat back in the grass as the partygoers hovered near the scene, gawking at Sam as if he were just part of the bigger show, as if his life didn't really hang by a thread.

Then his mother was there, talking in soothing tones, but he must have blacked out at some point. He couldn't remember everything that happened. "You did good, Kerry. They've got him now."

"Ok. I found him, Mom. He was at the bottom. He wasn't breathing. What happened? Where's Molly?" He stared ahead at the lights, heard the sirens turn on, felt all his muscles give way.

"She's with him. You're ok, son. You did good, baby. Do you need to get checked out?"

"No. I just need... I need to get warm. Is he alive, Mom?"

"They've got a pulse. They were working on him when they left. You did good, though. You got to him."

"I got to him in time?"

"Yes, love. Let's get you dried off and warm. Come now." He stood with his mom and walked up the hill toward the house. He saw Sunny out of the corner of his eye, directing Fran back to the kitchen, corralling her guests back toward the deck, resuming her social. And he heard her clearly say, "I knew using her was a mistake. He wasn't supposed to be any trouble."

Kerry bent down to pick up a pair of white high heels strewn on the lawn. He knew everything he needed to know at that moment.

"You ok, honey?"

"Yeah. It's just..." He pushed the shoes toward his mom. "She's gonna need these. Go help her, Mom. You can help her. I can't. I'll just be in the way."

"But you should..."

"Mom, don't. Go help Molly." He held the shoes out and placed them in his mom's hands. "I'll call you later. Besides, I've got to talk to Sunny."

SHE HAD NEVER FELT so panicked in her life. They'd taken him back into the ER, through the swinging double doors, away from her. She'd been directed to the front – to the cold vinyl chair in the waiting room, alone, her dress wet from his hair resting in her lap in the ambulance, barefoot after abandoning her shoes when she'd run toward Kerry's shouts, when she'd apparently lost the last good thing in her life.

And she knew how he felt. At that moment, she'd known why Kerry had been so apprehensive. No, not apprehensive. Petrified. The terror had been overwhelming. It had changed her. She might have lost the best part of her. An accident, yes. But it didn't change the guilt, the feelings of helplessness, the hurt.

"Mrs. Winters?" The nurse looked over the sea of other families, waiting for their news, or their turn, or their world to pivot.

"Yes. I'm Molly Winters." She stood and moved hastily toward the woman dressed in light-blue scrubs. Her nametag read "Maggie, RN." Molly felt the gentle weight of an angel on her shoulder.

"Your son, Sam..."

"Yes?"

"He's been stabilized, but he's still what we would call critical. He's not awake yet, but that's probably to be expected. He has a tube to breathe for him. We've started warming him up, and we're moving him to the ICU. He'll be in Room 312."

She fell to her knees, her face suddenly flooded with tears held back in the waiting. "Thank you. Thank you for saving him."

"Get up now. Come with me. He needs you to be strong up there. And we didn't save him. Whoever pulled him out at the scene saved him." Maggie helped her to her feet.

Molly nodded. "Yes. He did. I know. Can I see him now?"

"Go up to the ICU and tell them who you are. They'll let you through the doors, and it's family only up there."

"It's just me. I'm his family." Molly wiped the tears from her cheeks with a swipe of her hand.

"Well then, you better go up and be with him."

"Thank you again." She hugged the nurse, probably scaring her with the force of it, before she ran to the elevators, pausing only to scan the floor directory, confirming the ICU was on the third floor. Andrea Montgomery rushed through the front doors and up to Molly, enveloping her in a hug.

"He's in ICU. He saved him, Andrea. He saved him."

"Here, let's get this one." She directed her to an open elevator and pushed the button for three.

Once inside, Molly wiped at her tears again, trying her best to control her emotions before she saw her son. "Andrea, is Kerry ok? Did he get checked out?"

"He's fine, dear. He's worried about Sam. We are all worried about Sam. He didn't want to be a distraction here. And he doesn't want any praise for saving Sam. He just wants him to be ok."

"Oh, God. Let him be ok."

They ran out of the elevator, and Andrea directed her toward the pediatric ICU. With a swipe of her card, she opened both automatic doors. Molly felt like she was entering an alien ship with the beeping and the lights, with trepidation and fear of the unknown, of the unimaginable. They located his room, and she moved quickly to the side of his bed, where a nurse adjusted his IV lines.

"Can I touch him?" What a foreign idea to a mother.

"Of course. Hold his hand and tell him you're here. Oh, hello, Dr. Montgomery. Is this your grandson?"

"Not genetically. But he's very special to me, to my boys." She ran a hand over Molly's back as she took the seat at his bedside.

Molly gently slid her shaking hand under his limp fingers. She used the other to rub the top of his cold forearm, one that felt alien and utterly paralyzing. She kissed it in a vain attempt to let him know she was there, a mother's kiss to help him heal. "He's so cold."

The nurse answered as she adjusted the head of the bed with the controls on the end, "We are rewarming him as fast as we can. He has a tube to breathe for him, but you can see his strong pulse on the monitor there." She pointed to a small screen beeping in rhythm with his heart.

"Will he be ok? Will he come back to me?" Her voice, whispered out through raspy tears, didn't sound like her own.

"The doctors will be in very soon to update you. Do you need anything? Coffee? Water?"

"Thank you, no. I just need him to be ok."

The nurse rested a hand on her shoulder as she walked past. "He's working on it. Give him some time."

HE'D STALKED BACK TO the outdoor kitchen, where he watched Sunny order Fran to make up the remaining trays and serve the dessert. "Keep the Champagne flowing. They'll forget what they've seen."

He stepped up behind her. A sense of relief washed over him. "It's over, Sunny."

She seemed startled despite his calm tone. "Kerry, love. Go inside and change your wet things."

"I said, it's over."

"No, we can recover from this unfortunate event. I did not work this hard to have it all end over that kid. My social is not over." She started to run a hand over her blonde bob.

"That's not what I'm talking about. You and I..."

"You're talking nonsense. You're just shaken up from this ordeal. Trust me, I'm shaken up too."

"You're shaken up?"

"Kerry, go in and change. I'll get us back on track out here. Maybe, if you are suitably dressed when you return, we could announce our engagement. Yes, that could be just the thing to save the day."

He started to laugh...uncontrolled, unrelenting, unbelieving laughter.

"Have you lost your mind? Our friends are watching." She gave a beauty-pageant wave to a guest as they scurried past the tent.

"No, I haven't lost my mind. I've just gained some much-needed perspective. This...you and I...this is over. I don't give a flying rat's ass about your social, or our imaginary engagement, or your inflated ego, or these vapid, insincere people you call friends. That kid may not live, and you're worried about saving your image?"

She dusted a fictitious spot on her lapel and put a hand on her hip. "Is this about Molly? Because I don't see her rushing back to you for saving that kid. You're going to be alone, Kerry."

"No, let me make myself clear. As all things in your crystal bubble are, this is one hundred percent about you, Sunny. It is about how you treat people in this life. It is about grace. I'd rather be alone the rest of my life than spend another minute as your pet."

"I'm not going to have this conversation with you. Especially not here."

"You can have it with yourself anytime you like. I won't be here to hear it."

He heard the clapping in the distance – quiet at first and then louder as he made his way past the cheering guests and out toward his car. He didn't know if they were cheering because of what he'd done for Sam or what he'd said to Sunny.

Either way, he had somewhere to be.

The ICU at Children's Memorial was easy enough to find but, perhaps, was the most difficult of places to enter. The panel outside the ICU stated the rules – "Immediate Family Only." But that wasn't the issue. He simply couldn't put one foot in front of the other and actually walk through the doors. His mom found him outside the entrance.

"Kerry, what are you doing here? You should be home resting."

"I couldn't. I needed to see him...her. I needed to see for myself."

"I can let you in. Do you want to go in?" Her voice was consoling... It was her doctor voice. He'd recognized it from the years she'd brought him along on rounds or spoken to families on the phone when their kids were sick, suffering, dying. His stomach sank at the thought.

"Yes... No. I don't know what to do."

She took his hand. "Come inside. Then you can go from there." They walked through the double doors but stopped outside of Room 312. "I'll let you decide what to do from here."

"But it's family only in there." As if it were the arbitrary rule that kept him from pushing through the door.

"Sure is." She kissed his cheek. "Go ahead when you're ready. I'm going to get Molly some coffee." She patted his shoulder and walked down the long hallway from which they'd come.

He ventured a peek through the glass door. The curtain obscured half the space, but he could see that Molly sat next to the bed, her back to him, holding Sam's hand. Two doctors were talking near her, probably to her, but he couldn't tell what news they were giving. Their expressions appeared supportive, not panicked. Calm and controlled. *That is what she needs*, he thought. Not his driveling awkwardness. Not his stream-of-consciousness rambling. She didn't need any more emotion in that room.

He was no help here. He turned to lean his back against the wall, slid down to the floor in a crouch, listened to the steady sound of Sam's heartbeat on the monitor, and thought of his mom's hand in his. He didn't need to go in. She had been clear that she didn't need him in her life, that she didn't want what he was offering.

A nurse stopped in front of the door. "Are you family, sir?"

"I don't...I don't know."

"You'll need to move on, sir. You can't sit out here. The waiting room is right through those doors." She pointed down a long hall toward the front of the hospital. "There's coffee and chairs in there. Looks like you could use both."

He stood up slowly, rubbing his hands together nervously. "Thanks, I'll go."

"Want me to tell someone in here that you came by? Have them call you?"

"No, she's got enough to deal with. I'm sorry I took you away from Sam. You look busy. Thank you, though."

Later that night, after he'd taken two hot showers but still felt cold to his core, Kerry lay in bed, unable to find rest. It wasn't the cold. It was the loss. He finally knew what it was to love, and it was gone before he'd even recognized the feeling. He tossed and turned under the covers.

Sleep would not come. Not until he knew.

He thought about calling the hospital, but he didn't expect they would give him any information by phone. He thought to call Molly, but she'd made it clear that she didn't want to hear from him again. Finally, as he set the phone down for the tenth time, he got a simple text that changed everything.

Thank you.

He closed his eyes. The fear and the pain and the guilt left his body. And he slept.

Chapter 13

"YOU'VE GOT THE PRESS junket directly after the ribbon cutting. All the major news crews will be there. The reception will follow." Janie straightened his tie as she churned out the events of the plant opening.

"I hate ties and public events. Why did I pick this job again?"

"Because you love ships, and making things, and having the world's best assistant. Here is your speech."

"Right, of course." He looked down at the light blue index cards she'd given him and exhaled. He handed them back to her and pulled out a set from his jacket pocket. "I've written a different speech."

"That doesn't sound like a good idea. Do you need me to proof it?"

"No. Much to the surprise of both you and my mother, I'm capable of expressing myself without the assistance of others. But...thanks, Janie."

She sighed with pride. "Good luck today."

"I'm definitely going to need it."

Groups of reporters, city council members, and Montgomery Shipping employees all gathered in front of the new plant doors, where a bouquet of microphones had been set up for the announcements.

His gut hurt. He hadn't seen her yet. It would all be for nothing if she wasn't there to see what he'd done. No, that wasn't true. His company supported this city. He did what was right for the people of the city, not to win her back. But he'd take that bonus if he could get it.

"Janie, is Molly here with the catering? I haven't seen her."

"She arrived hours ago. I sent her back to set up in the main lobby. Why? Did you have something to say to her?" Janie's smirk was knowing.

"Can you get her out here for the announcements?"

She squeezed his hand. "On it, boss."

He found his parents near the podium and shook his dad's hand. "Son, you did good here. This is your project, your day. I'm not going to talk up there. This is not my legacy to claim. It's yours. I'm proud of you."

"Thanks, Dad. I appreciate that." His mom gave his arm a squeeze through his suit coat. "Are we ready to start?"

He stepped up to the microphones, completely out of his element, and perhaps out of his mind. He cleared his throat. "Ladies and gentlemen, thank you for coming today. We at Montgomery Shipping are proud to announce the opening of this new state-of-the-art plant along with the improvements to the port that will bring in so much to the city of Chicago, our home and yours. But we aren't here to simply cut this ribbon with some oversized scissors and eat cake." The crowd laughed. He smiled at Janie, who beamed about her joke and that he'd include it in his speech. He took the moment to look out into the crowd, scanning for Molly's blonde hair, her stunning blue eyes.

And then he saw her. She wasn't laughing with everyone else. She made no attempt to wave nor gain his attention. She was dressed simply in a black sheath, her blonde hair dusting the top of her shoulders, sadness filling her blue eyes. Within this crowd of hundreds, he focused on no one but her. He directed the rest of the speech at her alone, and he no longer needed his notes.

"We are here for much more than that today. Everyone has a story to tell. I was reminded of that recently. Mine started the day I realized that business isn't just about steel and ships. As much as I love the math and the details of this business, it can't be just about figures and lines on a graph. It has to be about people. It's about this city and everyone who lives here, even those who never get to tell their stories. So, today, we are proud to announce not only the opening of this plant, but the inaugural Chicago City Shelter Project. The plant will open as planned with employment for six hundred Chicagoans, many of whom will live in the new shelter built on this very corner. Our architect, Malcolm Allister, came into the project late, but he brought the idea to life quickly, and I think you'll see his innovation in every aspect. The Shelter Project is a collaboration between the City of Chicago and Montgomery Shipping, working toward permanent housing and stable employment for the one hundred and seventy-two men who currently call this corner home. They all have a story to tell, some of families and of broken systems, some of war and illness, most of strength and of love. We welcome them to the Montgomery Shipping family. Now, about this ribbon..."

The crowd applauded. His focus lay solely on Molly. Her reaction, her story was the only one that mattered to him. She smiled broadly, wiping a tear from her eye, and mouthed, *Thank you.* Kerry stepped up next to the ribbon and shook hands with a clean-shaven, overly thin man. He and Ken did the honors together.

SHE'D RUN BACK TO THE lobby to make sure the final food preparations were perfect. After all, now it wasn't just for the City Council or Montgomery Shipping. It was for her guys. She hugged Ken, barely recognizing him without his beard and fraying hair.

As she pulled back, her voice cracked with happiness for him and the men she'd cared about for the last few years. "You weren't kidding when you said you could look good in a suit. You clean up pretty well, my friend."

"So do you."

"I'm so happy for you and all of these guys." She hooked her arm under his.

"Listen, I owe you something. I'm sorry I doubted you, Molly. I should have known you were always on our side."

"You don't own me an apology, Ken. I have a sinking feeling that I owe one to your new landlord, though."

"Feels good to have a place to be, to call home. He's a good man. Hope he makes you Jolly, Miss Molly." He hugged her again before moving away toward the catered food, a little more skip in his step, a new chapter in his story.

"No show planned today?" It floated across the air on an Australian accent. "It's the main reason I came today, honestly. Not for the acknowledgment of my work, but because Mr. Montgomery said you'd be here. I didn't want to miss another performance."

She flushed with embarrassment, but she laughed too. She could laugh at herself. "It's nice to see you again, Mr. Allister, is it?"

"Call me Malcolm. After what I witnessed, I feel like all formality between us would be a sham at this point." He wrapped an arm around her shoulder and lowered his voice. "You know, love, we were making the changes to this place when you busted through that door. And even after that spectacle, I can tell you, he never looked back. I don't think he ever thought to cancel the project. Just thought you should know that. Now, I have to go sample this magic food I've heard so much about. And flirt with that pretty waitress there."

"Her name is Fran."

He moved away with a squeeze of her arm. "Well, here I come, Fran."

She laughed. He'd decided to change the plans before she'd busted into his space and before she'd pulled up stakes and rolled out of his life. And he'd never looked back. She realized now he'd been listening to her about these men and their stories. He'd been listening to her story. He hadn't done this to get her back or as a publicity stunt. He'd done it because it was the right thing to do and because he wanted to make her happy. There was no one in her life who wanted that for her. To her, that was love.

She felt him standing behind her from the electricity between them before she even turned around. He looked handsome – no, dapper was more appropriate – clean-shaven in his gray pinstripe business suit, black tie, and shiny shoes. As striking as he looked, she still preferred Saint Kitts casual on him – with his hair mussed from the breeze and a five o'clock shadow.

"Hey." She tried not to smile as she said it.

"Hey. Can we talk somewhere?"

She gestured to the area behind them. "That new kitchen is a pretty good place to start."

They walked quietly, without touching, back to the new shelter's kitchen, complete with new restaurant-grade equipment and a full pantry.

She turned back, unable to hold silent any longer. "It was a wonderful surprise, Kerry. Why didn't you tell me when I broke down your door in a fit? Malcolm said you were changing the plans in that meeting."

"Did Malcolm say that? Ratted on me pretty fast, I see. To be honest, I couldn't really get a word in at that point." He smirked at her.

She looked down at her feet with embarrassment for her behavior.

"But I was also a coward." Her eyes shot back up to his, grass green and ultimately clear. "I was too scared to tell you about my fears – to face them. So, I used the chance you gave me to end things."

Her chest hurt at the acknowledgment. Maybe he hadn't done this to make her happy. Maybe he didn't want to be with her after all.

"Well, thank you for doing it anyway." She pushed her hair behind her ear in a show of nervous energy.

"Your guys will be happy, I hope."

"I think so. And how about you? Will you be happy?"

"Am I one of your guys now?"

"That depends on you. Lucky for you, forgiveness is one of my top three traits." She smiled genuinely. She could forgive, but she couldn't move forward without a different path. "But I don't know that anything has changed. You said you couldn't be with us. You didn't want Sam."

"I did say that. I meant it at the time, but I didn't love him then. Or I should say that I didn't know that I did. Love changes everything. It changed everything for me." He moved forward and ran his hands over her bare arms, setting the hairs on end and sending electricity through her.

"When you saved Sam..."

"When I saved Sam, I saved myself – from a life without you and without him and this family. Love changed my heart. If I tell you I love you, will it change yours?"

"It already did."

Epilogue

"WHY ARE WE GETTING up at four thirty in the morning? We're on vacation." Sam flopped back onto the bed with a dramatic performance worthy of an Oscar. He continued to whine as she tossed a white t-shirt, button-down shirt, tie, belt, and khaki pants on top of him. "And I have to get dressed up? Why does dressing up always mean you have to put on extra layers?"

"It's just one of those mysteries of life, buddy. We're doing something special today, remember?"

"I remember," he huffed out as he pulled the blanket back up over his dark curls.

"I want you—"

"No harm in wanting, Mom..."

Molly couldn't help but laugh at his sass. He'd grown up so much in the last year. She told everyone he was now eight going on eighteen. "Sam, I want you to go change downstairs and meet Kerry in the living room in five. Don't forget to brush your teeth."

"I'm pretty sure I just did that like four hours ago."

"Do it again. Let's go."

He grabbed the clothes and shuffled to the bathroom, only to emerge a few minutes later still sleepy-eyed. "I can't get this tie on straight."

"I'll help you."

She watched from the balcony as Kerry kneeled in front of her son, reaching forward to adjust the tie and smiling at Sam.

"I have never gotten used to wearing these. Hey, I've got an idea. Maybe we should both take them off today. What do you say we roll up our sleeves and marry your mom in our own way? Let Drew and CJ wear the ties today."

"Can we really do that? I mean, Mom might get mad."

"I'll make sure she isn't. You make sure we're all set in the cars, ok? You've got best man duties today."

"Ok. I can do that." Sam started toward the front door but turned back after a few steps. He hesitated, "Hey, Kerry?"

"Yeah."

"I just wanted... I wanted to say thanks."

"For what, kiddo?"

"I never said a real thank you for saving me from the water last spring. I'm... I'm happy you're marrying my mom today."

"Me too."

She snuck away, letting them have their moment together. Jillian and Hailey were waiting for her in the bedroom. They helped her slip into the short lace dress for the ceremony – her something new. She'd found it in an island shop just this week. Nothing in Chicago had felt right; somehow, she'd known it would be waiting for her here in her new favorite place.

Hailey handed her the white high heels, the ones she'd worn to the social, the ones she'd discarded without hesitation when she'd run toward her son's limp body. They were her something old – old challenges, old feelings, an old life. She only needed them to get her to the beach. Once there, she'd abandon them for the feel of the sand underfoot. She wanted to be connected to this island when she married Kerry, feet solidly on the ground, her hands in his, with the sun rising on this new day and a little magic spilling into their lives.

She had chosen to wear her mother's emerald wedding ring on her right hand as her something borrowed. She and Jillian shared it now, but both women agreed it was borrowed from their mother's memory, their shared past, and their families' futures.

Michael married them. She proclaimed his Blue Banana van her something blue.

Sam walked her down the aisle. He stood by Kerry as his best man as she recited the vows she'd written.

"Kerry, I feel like everything in my life has led me to this moment, this place. My choices, my failures, my heartbreaks...everything brought me here. And when we are together, my past seems worth every minute of it. It brought me to you. I choose you. And I know, at this moment, that this choice is without pride, or selfishness, or regret. It is only with a heart filled with love and grace. I take you as my husband, my lover, and my friend. And I will every day going forward."

Kerry reached up and gently wiped a tear off her cheek. "That's better. Molly, you once tried to tell me that you didn't have anything to offer me. That our worlds, our lives, were too far apart. But you were wrong. We are here because your gifts abound, because you gave me the life, the story, I always wanted but was too afraid to go after. It's my turn to give something to you." He exhaled deeply. "Molly Anne Winters, with this ring and these vows, I give you my whole heart – the one you and Sam put back together with your love. I promise that from this day forward, you will not walk alone. I didn't fall into love with you. I walked into love with you, with Sam, with our families by our sides. I give you my love to be your nourishment. I give you my heart to be your shelter. I give you my arms to be your home. I walked into love, and it changed everything."

Standing ovation.

Her old friends watched her and Kerry join and transform into a new family all in the span of a sunrise.

They returned to the Montgomery house for an eclectic wedding brunch that included everything from cinnamon latte pancakes to mac n' cheese and even Chicago-style, deep dish pizza. So many personalities, so many delights.

When it was time to head home, back to the reality of Chicago and their lives, she felt no fear, no angst about what the future would bring. They had each other this time.

She'd walked into the Montgomerys' Saint Kitts home as a Winters. She'd be leaving the island as a Montgomery. Nothing felt more right. She had made a lot of choices in her life – to have Sam, to keep him at sixteen without his father to help her, to risk starting a business, to love Kerry Montgomery. Not every choice had led to perfect outcomes; life doesn't work that way. Some choices had been hard but worth the effort. Some choices had been easy – like saying yes to Kerry's proposal and marrying him on Sand Bank Bay Beach at sunrise.

Forgiveness had brought her here. Her choices in life had brought her here. Love had changed everything and brought her to this moment. She was determined to tell her story – not the one of her dad's sadness or the one of her mom's absence, but the one that had woven together the love of these families and changed everything.

Author's Note

THE CHICAGO SERIES saved my life.

I know that sounds cliché, and you don't have to believe me, but I'll always know the truth. *Waters' Reflection* started this journey back when I was still working as a physician. To combat burnout, I wrote on weekends, evenings after the kids went to sleep, and holidays – pretty much any time I could find, as many new writers do. Self-doubt often had me thinking, *Who cares about this? Why does this matter?* But the first book taught me, *Love Always Matters*.

I started to write *Powers' Pulse* before breast cancer diverted my days and nights with worry. I set it aside when my brain could not put two coherent sentences together while on chemo. I pushed it away when I was so tired during radiation that all I could do was nap and dream of finishing that book. It represents so much of me – the medical protagonist, the devoted mom, family-centered relationships, and it is dedicated to my breast cancer sisterhood. That book showed me *Love Finds a Way*.

Finally, when I had traveled that journey no one ever wants to take, I reached the summit of survivorship. *Winters' Season* is, for me, pure joy. It fell off my fingers in a way no other book ever has. It was all downhill because no one (and nothing — looking at you, cancer) could take it from me. I was a changed person, not because of cancer, but because of love. This third book promised me *Love Changes Everything*.

To me, these books are my miracles. They brought me back to who I am and who I wanted to survive to be. We are guaranteed nothing in this world. If my legacy remains my children and this series, I have reached the summit. My story has been told. and I am pure joy.

Like what you've read?

Join my group of amazing readers and friends at
www.jenniferdriscollauthor.com
Sign up for my newsletter for updates and new releases!

———————

Facebook more your thing?
www.facebook.com/jenniferdriscollauthor

———————

Maybe Instagram is your jam?
www.instagram.com/jenniferdriscollauthor

———————

Or my personal favorite, Pinterest? Take a sneak peek at the Montgomery Boys and their world through pins at
www.pinterest.com/jenniferdriscollauthor

About the Author

Jennifer Driscoll is one of those physician-turned-romance-novelists you are hearing so much about these days. She has special interests in suspense, life in the Midwest, classic wooden boats, Lake Michigan, and medical dramas. She attended the University of Notre Dame (Go Irish!) and Michigan State University College of Human Medicine. She is wife to Mr. Awesome, default parent to two sarcastic children, and a proficient killer of houseplants. She lives in beautiful Michigan with her family.

Read more at www.jenniferdriscollauthor.com.

97538896R00087

Made in the USA
Lexington, KY
30 August 2018